I0660136

ALEXANDER KAZARNOVSKY

WAR WILL TELL
THE FURTHER PLAN

London 2022

HERTFORDSHIRE PRESS

Published by Hertfordshire Press Ltd © 2022
e-mail: publisher@hertfordshirepress.com
www.hertfordshirepress.com

WAR WILL TELL
THE FURTHER PLAN

ALEXANDER KAZARNOVSKY

English

Editor Steven M. Bland
Translator Dana Zheteyeva
Typeset Alexandra Rey

British Library Catalogue in Publication Data
A catalogue record for this book is available from the British Library
Library of Congress in Publication Data
A catalogue record for this book has been requested

ISBN: 978-1-913356-49-1

ABOUT AUTHOR

Alexander Kazarnovsky born in 1951. Since 1967 he has been publishing poems, essays and poetic translations in the Moskovsky Komsomolets newspaper.

In the 1980s, he published the poetic translations of James Joyce, R. Frost, G. Longfellow, C. Brentano, F. Ruckert, as well as modern English, American and German authors.

His translations were published by the publishing houses: "Raduga", "Progress", in the supplement to the magazine, "Ogonyok,]", in the newspaper, "Moskovsky Komsomolets", and in the almanac, "Poetry".

In 1993 he immigrated to Israel.

His works were published in the periodicals: "Vesti", "Nedelya", "News of the Week", as well as in the newspaper "Panorama" published in Los Angeles.

In 2005, he published the novel 'Battlefield by the Moonlight' in Jerusalem. In the same year, he received the Jerusalem Olive Award for this novel in the Pages and Lines nomination. Circulation very quickly sold out in Russia, Israel and the United States.

In 2011, his second novel, 'The Four Wings of the Earth', was published.

Currently, his essays and stories are regularly published in the 'Novosti Nedeli' newspaper, on the websites "We Are Here", "Krugozor", and other periodicals and websites in Israel, the USA, Canada, Germany, Russia, and Ukraine.

His stories and essays were published in the collections called: 'Not Here and Not Now', 'Schisandra-1', 'Schisandra-2', 'Through the Eyes of the Heart', and 'Milky Way'.

He is a special correspondent for the Internet site "Krugozor" and a member of the editorial board on the site, "We are Schoolchildren".

In the fall of 2005, he published a book of essays called "Massacre".

His poems, essays, plays and stories were published in the "Limonnik" collections, as well as in the almanac "The Most Important Miracle", and other almanacs published by the "Helen Limonova Publishing House"

In 2021, his story "I Put Guards on your Walls" was published in the "New Journal", in New York.

Today he continues to write poetry, prose and essays and hopes that everything that the heroes of his novels dream about will one day come true.

In 2021, he became a laureate of the "Open Eurasia" competition (3rd Place) in the "Poetry" nomination.

WAR WILL TELL THE FURTHER PLAN

Guys, how should I wage this war? I am sitting on a roof and watching the object. He has a saddle-bag thrown over him like on a camel – they use those for carrying belongings… and he has children in those sacks… one in the front and one in the back. I am making an inquiry over the radio… I can take him out neatly in the head… I won't get the kids… I receive a negative response… he will fall and injure the children… do not shoot. And how should I wage a war with them then? I'm giving them the coordinates of the missile launcher; it's such a small truck, and it's in between buses filled with passengers… how can one fight in a war in such conditions?

The story of a sniper, a participant in the fighting in Gaza

The most curious thing was that there was no panic on the roof at all. On the contrary, it seemed that calm prevailed there. And it was not that apathetic tranquility of people who'd resigned themselves to violence, and who had nothing else to do other than wait for their destiny; it was live calmness mixed with interest. The attic door swung open and a hulk in a balaclava with a Hamas ribbon on his forehead pushed a young guy with short hair onto the roof. He was holding a crying baby in his arms, apparently his brother. It was clear that these ones, like Muhammad and Ahdaf and himself, were brought here involuntarily. But right after them, a flock of merrily laughing boys of about fourteen-years of age ran onto the roof too; obviously, nobody dragged them there. Moreover, they immediately started dividing up twenty-shekel notes and arguing animatedly; they'd clearly been paid to participate in this action. To the right of them stood a tall ginger-haired guy, whispering something inaudible and looking in the direction of the Israeli border. His cheek muscles were flexing visibly.

'Dad, are we going to die?' ten-year-old Muhammad asked suddenly.

Hamid hadn't managed to answer his son before the red-haired guy spoke instead.

'We will die, but THESE…' he waved towards the direction where the V-shaped drone hovering over the blocks came from, 'THESE should know — we are not afraid of them!'

'We'll die, but our death will contribute to the liberation of Palestine,' someone's voice was heard cutting through the sudden silence. 'The more of us die, the more support we will get all around the world!'

'And that will make the Jews retreat sooner,' another voice added.

'Dad, let's not die, let's go away,' Muhammad whispered, ardently squeezing his father's hand.

Little Ahdaf became sad let out a small sob. In response, a cry from the other side of the roof was made by the child who'd been brought there by his older brother, who in turn had been forced there by being poked in the back.

At that moment, the door opened once again and a few more people in overalls and balaclavas appeared on the roof. They were dragging plastic pipes, the type that are usually used for water pipelines or canal building. They started attaching three pipes to each other with insulating tape.

'Jump down their throats! Hinder them! Don't let them do it!' Hamid whispered to himself. But he did not jump or hinder. He let them proceed. Some weakness immobilised him as they quietly, even at a leisurely pace, finished what they were doing and returned to the attic door. This was all happening in complete silence that was infused only with the hum of the Israeli combat drone. Let it hum. As long as it hums, it seems the Jews will not shoot. The drone is their eyes.

'Jump down their throats! Hinder them! Kill them! Die yourself, but save your children! And those children standing on the roof not even suspecting what destiny has prepared for them. And those that are brainwashed and whisper curses towards Israel and are so desperate to die.'

The Hamas guys were already at the door when he made himself dash at them and cry: 'Wait! Where are you going? Let us go!'

And then something strange happened. The man, who was obviously in command of the others, suddenly stopped, turned around and took off his mask. He had a round face that was rimmed with an accurately trimmed black beard.

'You say let you go? Wait, soldiers, this one here wants us to let him go.'

These words sounded deceptively soft and gave him the power to shout:

'Let everyone, everyone go!'

'Everyone, you say? Hmm, I don't know about everyone, but we'll let you go, I think.'

'With the children…'

His voice, which had sounded so determined a second ago, now turned to pleading. It seemed as though something incredible was going to happen. That mercy would awake in the hearts of those hellhounds, those monsters, those Hamas people, and they would let go, maybe not everyone, but at least his children – Ahdaf and Muhammad.

'Ahdaf, Muhammad!' he cried, stretching his arms towards his sons.

'No, no, we didn't agree to that,' the owner of the short beard spat and punched him hard in the face. The pain from the punch mixed with the pain of the realisation he was being torn from his children and then the understanding that they were doomed. And it was all intertwined with Muhammad's cry: 'Papa!' and Ahdaf's sobbing.

Then everything disappeared — there were only stairs, stairs, stairs, stairs. Having belted down the flight of stairs flight, wiping the blood from his face, he made an attempt to get up. The "short-bearded" ran lightly down the stairs, grabbed him by the scruff of the neck and slapped his face, making Hamid tumble further down the stairs. Further and further. And every time Hamid stopped at the next landing, someone's boot sent him further on his journey down. This continued until he hit the bottom, and with a nonchalant gesture, the "short beard" took a remote control that could be suitable for a TV or an air conditioner from his pocket. He pressed the button. There was a noise that sounded like a jet plane when it flies right above one's head. Hamid looked up at the sky. That intertwined white thread cutting through the azure July, the thread that was stretched to nowhere, though no, not nowhere, but to the east, was saying silently: 'A response will fly back, a terrifying response! A response will fly back, a terrifying response! A response will fly back, a terrifying response!' Hamid dashed back to the entrance. Quick, upstairs, up! Of course, they would have locked the door to the roof, but he would break it down, bash it in!

Some of the security guards tripped him, and he stretched on the ground to the sound of their guffawing. Turning onto his back, he helplessly observed how the rocket exhaust was becoming wider and wider and wider in the ultramarine sky…

***

Moshe tipped back in his armchair, pressed the "disconnect" button on the remote, and his screen went dark. There had been times when citizens of Saad hadn't even dreamt of such technology. Then there was a general meeting where they discussed the question of whether inhabitants of the religious kibbutz could watch TV.

'That's it!' freckled Greenberg shouted. 'Now we have everything just like in a conventional kvutsa. Soon, we'll get to the times when there will be common showers and bedrooms for boys and girls!'

"No, we won't!" a majority of vote of the meeting decided, and decreed to start purchasing TV sets.

It was a long time ago…

Moshe closed his eyes. Thirty-five. IDF's thirty-fifth soldier killed since the beginning of the "Operation Strong Cliff".

Thirty years ago in Lebanon, they all were your brothers. Now — they are your sons, although you've never seen them. A brother's death is insanely difficult, but a son's death is excruciating. His right armpit is burning. It's some skin rash, probably caused by the deodorant. Cool stuff that "TITANIUM metal." That issue was also solved in a kibbutz with a row where Greenberg had been inquiring: 'Can an orthodox Jew perfuse himself with a scented spray, like a woman?' To which Rav Benjamin had replied: 'He can.'

It burns. He should go to the kitchen and get a soothing ointment, but he's too lazy to get up. His eyes are closed, but there is no darkness. The day is sunny indeed. And you understand that everything is red in your eyes just because the light is breaking through your eyelids and there are blood vessels there... well, and so on. You understand that well, but you still have a feeling that when you open your eyes now, there will be an ocean of blood approaching your eyelids. And those clocks. The one that's on the table and the one on the wall, they are honestly driving me mad with their cacophonic timbre and rhythm. Well, this big one on the wall, it doesn't tick, it tuts.

Twenty years ago, when they had the twentieth anniversary of their acceptance into the kibbutz with Dwora, they'd received that clock as a gift from the administration. If only you could hear how their kibbutz fellowmen of all ages shouted 'Mazel tov!' There were those who grew up in front of them and those who grew older before their eyes. And the clock was so pretty – the clock-face like an ocean with continents floating in it, and the second-hand a plane that was travelling across all those continents. Along the perimeter of the hour plate, there were the names of cities with little windows, where you could see what time it was in Paris or New York.

And the other clock that was not tutting but tapping — it had been bought by Moshe not so long ago. As he was the elder of the synagogue, he had to get up at an unearthly hour to open the synagogue, which is not that easy at sixty-four, and one could certainly oversleep. Besides, the alarm on the phone worked one day and didn't the next, so he'd had to buy that monstrous clock.

The mobile phone which lay on the little table and the sound of which Moshe, as usual, had forgotten to turn back on after he'd switched it to quiet mode during his prayer at the minyan started buzzing and humming weakly.

'Hello?'

Arye's voice sounded as if it was coming from a deep cave.

'Moshe…'

And pause. A pause which was wearying and seemed as if it could last for an eternity.

'Arye, what happened?' Moshe asked, although he already realised WHAT had happened. His memory briskly brought up the downhearted face of the snub-nosed, blue-eyed lady announcer… 'During the liquidation of the terrorist who was trying to find his way to our territory from Gaza, an officer of the Israel Defense Forces fell in battle.' The girl did not announce the name. According to the rules, first, they informed the relatives of the deceased. And it seemed as if they did inform them. Or did they?…

There was sobbing, then silence on the phone.

'Arye… Shimon?'

It seemed as if his lip cracked when he pronounced the name of that boy whose circumcision ceremony he'd attended twenty-seven years ago, and where he'd drunk a little too much and danced more merrily than anybody else; at whose Bar-Mitzvah he was summoned to the Torah as if he was related to the subject of the occasion, though he wasn't a relative but only the closest friend to the boy's father; at whose wedding, eight years ago, at the age of fifty-six, he was dancing with zest with the groom on his shoulders, and then as a badchen – a wedding entertainer – standing in front of that groom on his knees and leaning his body back so the back of his head was almost touching the floor while holding a burning torch on his nose…

'Arye…'

'The funeral is tomorrow at four o'clock,' he could hear the voice from the bottomless cave proclaim. Then there was silence.

Moshe slumped into an armchair. Then it was Shimon, indeed.

He didn't know how long he sat like that, staring at the dark screen of the TV set where nothing but his face and lacklustre eyes seemed to be reflected. A siren wailed and he could hear the stomping of feet and hurled shouts outside. Moshe didn't move. Then another "hello from Gaza" thundered, shot down by the "Iron Dome." A bell rang. Automatically, he brought the phone closer to the ear and heard Dwora's voice. Dwora's crying.

'Moshe, did you watch the news?'

'Arye called me,' Moshe whispered.

'Moshe, it's awful; yes, awful!" Dwora lamented. 'Moshe, there in Saad where the siren wails several times a day, it's all perceived differently. And here, in Pardes Hanna mothers with children may calmly fiddle around in playgrounds where elderly people sit on benches during the day, and where at night young men and girls sit and drink vodka, and where one can never, right, never hear either the sirens or the explosions… If a man looks up at the sky here, it's only because he wants to check if any cloud could mitigate the frigging heat… Here, a piece of news from the front is like a message from another planet, yes, from another planet.

And all of a sudden, that planet devours Shimon, right, Shimon…'

Moshe was silent, just as Arye had been not long before. He was much closer to Arye now, and maybe even to Shimon, rather than to Dwora. He was almost on another planet. Crying was a human's privilege. That's why he cleared his throat and said dryly:

'The funeral is tomorrow at four, Dwora. So, to-morrow I'm… Dwora, I don't want to escape from the kibbutz, I don't wanna do it at all, especially now, after Shimon's death. Through this pain, I can clearly feel that each of us must be in our own places. You're a dif-ferent case. You're in the right place — in quiet Pardes Hanna saving our grandchildren from bombings and maybe from death. And what about me? I'm here in the religious kibbutz, an elder of the synagogue, our synagogue. My thing is to arrange prayers, collect do-nations for the wounded soldiers and peaceful citizens, take care of people overloaded with problems and make sure they don't stop learning the Torah.'

Again, there was silence on the line, but this time it was a different silence — the silence of the unexpect-ed estrangement that emerged between a husband and a wife.

'But what about me? Yes, me?' Dwora asked in a low voice.

'Dwora,' Moshe pronounced, feeling that his throat was getting dry, 'you're engaged with our grandchildren. You're herding our little bandits. And I — I must be here, in my place. We are, of course, on different planets, but this… it doesn't hinder me from loving you as much as I've loved you for the last years, for all these last years, not stopping for a minute.'

He felt that the woman on that other planet was smiling through her tears.

After talking with his wife, he silently stared out the window at the orange gardens, at the crooked acacia, at the sand hills, the crescentic dunes and the cypresses of the kibbutz. So what, should he just sit there idly? He had a remedy for that, and it was always helpful when he felt that his heart was in his throat. He would get into his Subaru and drive to the sea. Piercing into the eternity of the sea that was ultramarine during the day and black with the silver brim of the breaking waves at night, he felt another eternity — the eternity of the One who created that sea, and the Earth, and him — Moshe Abu. "Have you created me? Then help me!" And the Eternity always responded: "Yes."

* * *

The water in the tunnel was up to the sheen. "The further I go, the worst it would get," Hamid thought. "Though, no. It's summer now, and I'm at the edge of the desert. There shouldn't be any water here. Water, disappear!"

The quaintest thing was that as soon as Hamid pronounced these words inside his head, the puddle under his feet started becoming shallow, and, in a few meters, dry sand started crunching there instead of it. And no wonder, the ceiling and the floor of the tunnel now sharply curved up, and Hamid even felt that he was a little out of breath.

Well, yeah, there are good grounds for saying: "One cannot dig a well with a needle." And here, even if they didn't dig with a needle, who dug it? Boys of about twelve? Apparently, these boys were sick and tired of brandishing a pickaxe here, or maybe it was hard to work and drag themselves uphill. The tunnel became narrower. Narrower is not even the word for it. In some places, one almost had to squeeze through. That is, if Hamid was a bit fatter, he would definitely have to squeeze himself through. Say, take that fat Yaser Tirawi, he wouldn't get through at all.

Hamid walked and walked and walked. The main thing was not to close his eyes. As soon as he did, he saw that dead boy, the one who lay back there at a damp concrete wall, all hunched up. The crucial thing was to think about some petty things and not about that boy or any other boys, not about the scariest things. And, of course, not about Ahdaf and Muhammad. But how could he not think about them if they were always before his eyes…

Sweat was not simply running down his cheeks, Hamid thought that he was bathing in his sweat. He didn't have enough air. His head was spinning. The light ring reflecting from his torchlight was dancing and trembling ahead of him. He realised this was happening because his hands were shaking. He was this close to losing consciousness and falling… and he would doze off and be over and never come back to his senses. He would lie there all hunched up and soon become cold. Without stopping, Hamid took a one-litre plastic bottle from his bag and started drinking the water greedily, spilling the precious liquid. It gave him strength, though not for long. He hadn't lasted for another kilometre when he felt he was tripping over his feet again, and the light ring was doubled… tripled…

He crouched down on the ground, slipped his hand into the pocket of his pants, and checked whether the Instruction, which was as precious as water, was still there. His soles were sore, as were his ankles and knees. And Taufik had warned him: 'Don't go into the tunnel! Let's say it straight, you won't be able to do it. You won't get through. As they say, stretch out your legs along the length of your carpet.' And he had kept a bold face, saying: 'For the sake of seeing Ulenspiegel, I will go through.' For the sake of seeing Ulenspiegel... He needed to get up, but he didn't have the strength. For the sake of seeing Ulenspiegel... It was so cosy and nice sitting there. For the sake of seeing Ulenspiegel... And it seemed that his head wasn't spinning anymore. Well, it did, but almost unnoticeably. For the sake of seeing Ulenspiegel... Hamid realised he had a choice — whether to get up or die. He wasn't at all afraid of dying, it wasn't painful — it was even comforting. But he had no right to die, he had to get up, get up for the sake of seeing Ulenspiegel.

Instruction... Instruction... Instruction...

***

In winter, in rainy weather, when you walk along the deserted beach, you might have a feeling there is a swamp beneath your feet. Not right under your feet though, but somewhere deep below... Somewhere there, under the crust of sand that pretends to be hard soil, the Bog, the Mud is waiting to devour you when you get further and deeper. But in summer, the sand is dead. It's not even sand at all; it's coarse dust. And Moshe, walking in sandals on his bare feet, lifts his head, and stares at the countless stars that seem to him to be God's eyes and whispers: 'Hello, God; here I am again. I came to You as I feel bad again. It's not that I forget about You without it; no. Three times a day I go to the synagogue and three times a day I whisper: "Blessed be You Almighty, our God and God of our fathers, God of Abraham, God of Itzhak, and God of Jacob." But when I feel bad, I come to the sea. I come to the other You, to the Father who bends before his son stooped under misfortunes. To the Father that strokes his soul with moist fingers, with the fingers of the waves, washing off the blood — the blood of the boy Shimon, at whose bar mitzvah I was dancing once, the blood of dozens of Jewish guys and the blood of dozens of Arabic children, innocent kids that have to pay for the crimes or silence of their parents. And my blood, my own blood that trickles down my soul, from the soul that's unable to bear the many-millennia-old burden of murders, murders, murders… The cat from the Passover song, "Chad Gadya" eats a goatling, a dog blows the cat to blazes, a stick breaks the dog's head open, fire destroys the stick, water puts out the fire, and above all this, the Death angel does not stop his dancing and will dance until You, Almighty, stop the circling of that merry-go-round, the bloody merry-go-round, and send us someone who will stop that vortex, that helluva vortex. How long can we stand it? How many years, how long have I been living in this world, and the darkness only thickens, terrifying darkness! And sometimes it seems that every perished person in the world is me, me, and that I and no one else am to blame for each of their deaths.'

The sand was dead, but the sea was alive. The sea was warm. The sea was breathing warmth. Having soaked in that boundlessness, Moshe started to read his evening prayer. Having reached the Eighteen Blessings, he rose from the barrier wall, turned to face Jerusalem, and with his back to the sea so the sea wind was caressing the back of his head, he spoke: 'Blessed be You, Almighty, our God and God of our fathers,

God of Abraham, God of Itzhak, and God of Jacob…'

When he reached the words, 'Hear the voice of ours,' he thought that somewhere in the heavens a huge ear opened. And he whispered into that ear: 'Dear Lord, bring the Deliverer to the Earth, and until then, Heavenly Father, derail plans for the dividing of Jerusalem and the expulsion of the Jews from their houses, and return Gush Katif and Northern Samaria to us. Avert the nuclear attack from us and the threat of a huge war. Help us make it so that the massacre here in Gaza stops soon so that as few people as possible perish — Jewish and Non-Jewish, Arabs and Non-Arabs. Make it so that children don't die, and we defeat those who rose up to destroy us. Dear God, enlighten the blind, enlighten the blind who dream of destroying my state; let them understand that by killing us, they are killing themselves.

Dear God, let my children be healthy and happy, and let my grandchildren live a long and happy life, and stay as faithful Jews forever.

'Dear Lord, accept Shimon's soul, Arye's son, who consecrated Your Name with his death. He was more vehement than an eagle and more powerful than a lion, fulfilling Your will. Take revenge for his spilled blood. Let his soul be a link in the chain of eternal life together with Abraham, Itzhak and Jacob, Sarah,

Rivka and Lea, and other righteous people whose souls are in the paradise.'

The prayer was over, and it was as if the pain from the soul was spent and a warm sea wave washed his soul. The sea kept silently staring at him. While he was reading the prayer, it completely calmed. Even the foamy rim disappeared — and just tongues of the tide gently licked the sand on the beach like a dog before retreating to the depths.

A siren wailed. A missile flashed up in the sky like a meteor and shot in the direction of Ashkelon. Right at the same moment, another meteor tore out from the darkness towards the first one — a fiery spit from the "Iron Dome." Blast — and somewhere in the distance, in the north, sparks and burning pieces of the missile showered from the skies.

Moshe noted with surprise that he was standing in the middle of the beach quite far from any shelter and was not at all scared. The all-seeing God was looking down at him with such fondness that it was clear nothing evil could happen to him.

He walked back on the shore along the parapet by the closed stalls and restaurants, and suddenly stopped. The distinct smell of cigarette smoke was in the air. Moshe turned around, but there was nobody there. That was weird. If he told anyone the air on the beach was filled with cigarette fumes, they would twist a finger at their temples. In the meantime, he started ascending the worn-out stone stairs to the gas station where he'd left the car.

***

From the portrait that covered almost half of the wall, a man in a tall black hat with his hair in disarray and long curly locks familiar to Hamid from comical pictures in newspapers issued in Gaza which were called, as he remembered, "payot" was looking down at him with amazingly piercing eyes that could make one jump bolt upright and report on all the good things and, Allah forbid, bad deeds one had committed during their life. Next to it, there was another picture of a crowd in jellabiyas led by a bearded fanatic indicating the way to a bright future; they were approaching the sea, which was obediently splitting apart in front of them with such speed that surprised fish were petrified in the left and right walls of that water.

Hamid looked at the pictures and ate. He ate the shakshouka that Moshe had made. He ate couscous and pita bread with tahini. He ate and still couldn't become full. For many days he'd had no possibility of eating decently, and to be honest, he'd had no desire to. Following Aya's death, he'd had to boil, fry, and bake for his children all by himself... And what do you know — food lost its taste for him. It seemed he was cooking the same recipes, but the food turned out completely different. He got the impression that Aya had added one more ingredient into the ommuali or buns with farmer's cheese, and it was called 'love.' No, he, Hamid, of course, loved his precious children, and how could he not love them? But he couldn't add love to his dishes. And after the boys perished, it was like blasphemy to take care of his nutritional needs, and, moreover, cook for himself. Sometimes, he would buy himself fruit or vegetables with the remaining money. Sometimes, mainly during yet another brief truce that Gaza occasionally enjoyed during the "Operation Strong Cliff", he'd go to a café and eat something with meat.

There was less and less money left, but Hamid didn't care about that. Having buried his entire family, he didn't care about anything at all and was ready to die and even meet his death with joy. During the academic year while teaching at school, if only classes weren't interrupted because of the war, he probably could have distracted himself a little and obtained some meaning for his existence that would help him stay afloat instead of sinking to the bottom. Now it was the summer vacation, however, and he was inevitably approaching his end. If anything was heartening to him at all, then it was his faith in the fact that one day he would find someone who would help him tell his story and show that terrible Instruction. For there should be a reason why this had happened to him; there should be a reason why Allah made him devoid of his Aya and the children. Allah was wise; Allah would ensure that all of Hamid's sufferings would have some meaning.

'And can you imagine…' Hamid sipped some coffee and continued his narration. The Jew was listening attentively and looking at him with his bright, dog-like eyes. 'Can you imagine, I managed to find him. I found Ulenspiegel; the real one! I didn't really find him personally, but… Can you imagine? I was digging in the wreckage of the newly destroyed building looking for something to eat… And, as ill-luck would have it, I found nothing but an open bottle of coke and some croutons. And suddenly, I came across a piece of newspaper. It looked like American, and the headline, oh, listen to it: "Stuttgart journalist Herman Schroder ('Ulenspiegel'): Pain, blood and ashes of Shudjaia are pounding in my heart!" As I read it… Can you imagine?'

'I can imagine,' Moshe said gloomily. 'The only thing is…'

'What?'

'What kind of an alias is "Ulenspiegel?" He hasn't come up with it yesterday or today, right? Shudjaia is pounding in his heart; well, let it pound! And what was pounding there before? It looks like it's some professional ash-pounder, some heart ash-pounder.'

Hamid gritted his teeth. In the end, this Jew provided him with food and shelter, and the fact he didn't believe in anything good in men… well, he was a Jew, after all. It was good that he hadn't told him about the Instruction. He wouldn't tell him anything. He'd speak only with Ulenspiegel and wouldn't tell anybody else.

'And what was that article about?' Moshe asked.

'Well, he wrote about our ordeals. He wrote them in blood. But who is to blame for all our misery…'

'Did he forget; did he forget to write about it?'

'The end of the article was torn away. Then I decided I'd find that journalist and tell him the truth about Shudjaia.'

'Nothing more, nothing less?' Moshe asked, curling his lips sorrowfully.

'And nothing more, nothing less,' Hamid replied firmly.

'Good,' Moshe said in a reconciliatory manner.

'But why would you go personally? There is email or Skype after all…'

'But you don't understand,' Hamid said, starting to get annoyed. 'When you speak about the main thing, about the most important thing, you need to say it looking straight into their eyes, face-to-face. And who would believe it in an email?'

'What about Skype?'

'I thought about that: from Gaza via Skype… I haven't had a computer for a long time, and connecting from someone else's computer would make that person open to a mortal blow.'

'And from here?'

'From Israel? They'd say it's a Jew disguised as an Arab. No, it needs to be eye to eye.'

'And for you, the most important thing in your life now is to tell them?'

'Is there anything else? They took from me everyone I loved.'

'Hamid, I'm sorry that I'm going to ask you this… err… stupid question — do you want to get back at Hamas?'

'No,' Hamid said wistfully. 'I don't want revenge; I want to stop them.'

'Okay. By the way, how did you rake up the money for the trip?'

'That was easy. I sold the apartment.'

Indeed, he said that so casually that Moshe realised everything and exclaimed:

'So, you're homeless now, right?'

'It looks like it,' Hamid replied in the same tone and smiled, probably for the first time since the day of his sons' deaths.

'Did you get much for your apartment?'

Hamid felt it was ridiculous. What could he get for an apartment that could be blown up if not today, then tomorrow; where the majority of the inhabitants were unemployed and those who worked hadn't got their wages in months? And Hamid didn't mention the main thing, that the Hamas soldiers taken away the money for that apartment a long time ago. That money that was tucked into a plastic bag together with his fake passport and the Instruction, as well as the money he bought this passport with was of a completely different origin. But he had no right to tell anybody about it, even if it was an enemy of Hamas.

'And how did you… manage to get here?' Moshe continued his naïve interrogation.

'I mean, through the tunnel. Look, you're fighting against those tunnels, however, but for that tunnel I wouldn't have had a chance to be able to get here alive.'

'Well, as far as I understand, you're too excited about those tunnels.'

'And who's arguing? It's horrendous! People were just grabbed and forcefully brought to build those tunnels without any safety measures at all. How many people were buried there? And children too. How many kids were enticed by the payment — one dollar an hour! How many were executed to keep the location of those tunnels secret? I saw the bones there. Those scoundrels didn't even bother to remove the corpses. I saw a dead boy. Nevertheless, it's thanks to that tunnel that I'm here.'

'Well,' the Jewish guy sneered. 'First of all, you're here thanks to the Almighty, and secondly... secondly, and please don't consider me an arrogant person, thanks to me, a little bit.'

Hamid nodded.

'It's owing to your yarmulke even more, the white one with little holes which I took for a taqiyah, just like yours at that gas station.'

'Took for what... for what?'

'For a taqiyah, an Arabic lacy skullcap, they're also white, just like yours.'

'And you, how on Earth did you appear at the gas station in the first place?'

'Where else could I go? I crawled out from the

underground in the middle of an empty beach, and my only hope was to find some Arab who could help me. The main thing was not to come across some Jew who would turn me in to the authorities.'

'Of course, how could you know there are normal people among the Jews, too?'

'Stop mocking me. We're not crazy. Yes, there are fanatics among us, for them ALL Jews are the descendants of pigs and monkeys, and that's why those so-called radicalised Muslims attack Jewish companies, museums, or restaurants all around the world, though the people that die there don't have any connection to Israel... but there's just a small group of those fanatics... the rest...'

'Right, of course, the rest just adore us.'

'Nobody adores you. The rest think there are Jews and there are Zionists. Jews are those who sit quietly and pray, preferably in Paris or London, and even let them be — Allah is merciful — in Jerusalem; only let them not claim our lands, not take away our lands, and not establish their state here.'

'I see, and Zionists, Zionists are those who claim your land and establish their own state here. Well, congratulations — right in front of you is not a quiet Jew who prays in Paris or Jerusalem, not a dhimmi that you agree to tolerate, but the Zionist, the religious Zionist!'

Hamid cringed at his words. It seemed as if he had an opportunity to disappear, to evaporate, to dissolve into the atmosphere, he would have reckoned it as a huge stroke of luck. And then Moshe's voice sounded again:

'Just chill, alright? I'm not poisonous at this time of the year, and I'm not going to turn you in to Shin Bet.'

'But why?' Hamid inquired. 'What if I am an inside terrorist?'

'If...' Moshe replied, 'or if not; what if you are telling the truth? And I would condemn the man, the man who has lived through the loss of his wife and three children to torments, to new ordeals, and, to be exact — to death. Think, what can await you with our police? They'll send you to prison for further investigation and put you in a cell, a cell with other Arabs. And who are you to them? A defector! You're a traitor!'

'But I didn't betray anybody,' Hamid rebuked Moshe. 'I was running away from Hamas. And do you know how we hate Hamas?'

'I don't, but I can imagine. I bet you hate them as they're throwing you under our missiles openly and forcibly and trying to lay their way to victory with the corpses of your children. But your brothers in Judaea and Samaria...'

'Where?'

'Those places you call the Western shore... and in Israel itself, there are masses of Arabs who worship those bastards. Well yeah, the Hamas soldiers don't throw local Arab children under their bombs. Timid Israeli policemen who can be spat at, poked with knives, have stones, firecrackers and Molotov's cocktails hurled at them stand up against local Arabs, and for that, they get hard cash from the same Hamas or Fatah. And there is almost no risk, because if the policemen punch back a bit harder, all our local rights activists, Jewish rights activists, and after them Jewish news people and newsreaders will tear them apart, no mercy, worse than Hamas soldiers, the most violent Hamas soldiers. None of the Nazis would ever hate a Jew as much in his life as a Jew would hate himself. And as for your Palestinian and even Israeli compatriots, they would never forgive your escape; no, they won't, don't pin your hopes on that. And the police wouldn't care — they wouldn't put you in the same cell with Jews. It would be better if you were in a solitary cell, but one needs to deserve it, and you're not worth it; you don't really look like a high-value criminal. Thus, you don't need to be in prison.'

'I mean, I'm not eager to go there!'

'You shouldn't be. And I'm going to say this to

you — when you told me about the children's death, I realised that it's either truth, and I would be a piece of shit, the last piece of shit if I turned you in, or you're a grand actor, and I have no right to destroy such a talent.'

'And what if I'm not just an actor, but also a terrorist?'

'You?'

Moshe burst out laughing. It was clear that the wine had made his head spin a bit and loosened his tongue.

'You are a terrorist? Just look at you! One can blow you away with a feather. You just tell me how fun it was for you when I told you in the car I was taking you to a Jewish village?'

Hamid squeezed out a smile.

'Well, I crawled to the gas station, saw an Arab in a taqiyah, asked him where he was going, and he responds: "To Saad." And I thought it was an Arabic name that means "Happiness." How do you know Arabic so well?'

'How could I not know it if I was born in Iraq!? So, it's real happiness, your happiness that you didn't come across a real Arab, otherwise, you would have experienced "Saad." You're right — my yarmulke should be bowed at to the last thread.'

'That's what I was thinking — how could I go to the airport with such an appearance, all dirty in rags? The police would... I should go and address the people in Saad and ask them for help...'

'Well, the people in Saad can indeed help you with clothes, at least one of them... that is me. By the way, do these trousers fit you well?'

'Yes, thank you.'

'What, "thank you?" What are you mewling for? I see they're a bit too long. Ok, just roll them up. Roll them up for now, and later we'll crop them. Well, so be it; I'll pick some clothes for you. And what's with the money and documents?'

'I've already bought a fake passport; you can inform the police.'

'I won't, I won't inform anybody. Only it's not right. Let me take you tomorrow to a journalist I know. He's ours, a rightist. He will do an interview with you.'

"Why not?" Hamid thought, caving in for a second in his mind. "Today's egg is better than tomorrow's chicken. And I could give the Instruction here, too. But, no. Who would believe in the authenticity if it was presented in Israel? And then...'

'No, Saidi Moshe,' he said firmly. 'We're still enemies. You're fighting against us. I'm very grateful to you. You helped me and probably saved me from the police. You picked me up on the road — I don't even know what would have happened if it wasn't for you. But it doesn't negate the fact that there's a war going on. There is a war, and to be published in your newspaper would mean switching to the enemy's side. Then you'd better turn me in to the police — I won't resist. I don't need any of your journalists, neither left nor right. I need just one person — Herman Schroder, Ulenspiegel.'

'I told you already that I won't take you to the police; I won't. But let's at least find the phone number of your Schroder via the Internet. Otherwise it's going nowhere… Do you have money, a lot of money?'

'I mean, enough for the first few days.'

'And what next, what about after that?'

Hamid shrugged his shoulders.

'And what if you don't find him straight away? Maybe he left for somewhere, for New York or say, Shanghai from his Stuttgart base for a month or two. He's a journalist, after all.'

'Well, I'll dig something up.'

'War will tell the further plan?'

'Wh-what? What plan?'

Moshe laughed.

'I'm originally from Iraq, and my wife is from Russia.'

'Really?' Hamid was surprised. 'Well, my friend who used to live in Shudjaia, his wife is from Russia. I don't know what her name was back home, but here she took the name Zakiya.'

'And how does she get along with the relatives, the Muslim relatives?' Moshe asked.

'At first it was difficult, but all the conflicts were solved with time. And she is a senior there, as her husband is the oldest son. And they're both doctors. And even though she doesn't work in the hospital, everyone runs to her to get injections. Or she comes to them to make infusions. She also goes in for swimming and fitness, and she cooks Russian food, which wins everybody over. She has a diploma as a pastry cook; she bakes cakes. Yummy! There is a special one called a "Napoleon."'

'And where is your friend now?' Moshe asked.

'Well, they moved to Rafah. There's almost no bombing there.'

'Yeah,' Moshe mumbled. 'It's pretty shitty for us and for you, too. War is a freaking, freaking thing.'

'And how are you a-a-an Iraqi... Jew,' Hamid squeezed out that word with difficulty, 'who managed to marry a Russian girl? And where is she?'

'She's in Pardes Hanna with our grandchildren, and I'm here with you relapsing into drinking and rampancy. I got acquainted with her in Bnei Akiva. It's a sort of organisation, a religious youth organisation for Zionists, by the way. So, in such cases my wife has a saying, a Russian saying — "war will tell the further plan." Meaning that we will get into a war now and then act based on the situation according to the circumstances. Looks like you reckoned the same, that war will tell the further plan.'

'Generally, yeah, something like that. Anyway, I'm so grateful to you — you helped me a lot and all… but please, don't consider me your ally. On a larger scale, I don't see the difference between Hamas and the Israel Defense Forces.'

Moshe rose slowly and approached Hamid, who was finishing yet another cup of coffee, put his hand on his shoulder and said in a low voice:

'To tell you the truth, I don't see anything in common. And you should remember one thing: in the IDF, the commander will never order his warriors: "Forward!" There is no such order there. The order is: "Follow me."'

"What has that got to do with anything?" Hamid thought.

***

So that was how it was happening on the other side. First 'uuuhh!' and then 'Boom!"

'That's "The Dome,"' Moshe commented. 'The "Iron Dome."'

Two hours later, after yet another "boom," he entered the room to Hamid, who jumped up from the bed and explained: 'Don't worry, that rocket of yours blew up in an open field. I passed such a place two days ago,' he added. 'A stray dog was killed by a fragment. It was horrible. All its guts were inside out.'

"It's horrible," Hamid sullenly thought as he looked at the white yarmulke in the dark, "but you haven't seen true horror."

Having guessed his thoughts, Moshe smirked:

'I was in the war in Yom Kippur, in Yom Kippur in 1973, and in Lebanon before that. I've seen enough of even worse things. My friend died in my arms, and I saw a girl, a Christian girl who'd been hacked to death together with her family. But God forbid me from living to the day when I have no more tears for a dog, for a stray dog. Alright, the attack is over. I'll go back to my room to sleep.'

It was only when a snore was heard from the

other room that Hamid thought: "Whenever there's a siren, he runs to this room — the heder bitahon (safe room) as he calls it, even when he speaks Arabic. Until I turned up, he probably slept in this room, protected, and now he's given it to me."

Hamid went to the window. Low streetlamps were lined up along the road, staring at the ground with their round, yellow-orange eyes. The undersized palm trees were moving their spread-out, pointy fingers in the scant light. Behind them, there were low, flat-topped houses that looked as if they were drawn decorations. It was a boring view. All of a sudden, a wild thought piercing his brain literally shook Hamid up. Waves of blood were pouring down his motherland, and he was there drinking coffee with… with whom? With a murderer, indeed. What was that Moshe saying? "I fought in Yom Kippur and first in Lebanon." Fighting — that means he was killing there.'

There was silence behind the window. A heavy silence. Dusty air and a dusty silence. The mouldy silence of someone else's settlement and someone else's life. A car passed by. No, it didn't pass by; it stopped next to the house opposite. It was a strange car. For some reason, a blue signal was spinning on its roof… Allah is great — that's the police! Oh, Hamid-Hamid! You are too relaxed. You trusted your enemy, and here's the result: as they say, you were running away from the rain and got caught in the torrent. Of course, the Hamas guys were scoundrels, but they were your fellow troops. And here, that 'heder bitahon,' he'd let his guard down. He'd forgotten that even the prophet Muhammad called the Jews liars; indeed, it says in the fifth surah of the Quran: "Do not consider Jews and Christians as your supporters and friends." It was a good thing he hadn't shown him the Instruction. What should he do? How could he find a way out? Right, the way out from the house to the backyard. Where is that back door?

Hamid quickly grabbed the clean clothes Moshe had prepared for him and put them on a chair.

"Gosh, how caring he is — right, of course, he was doing it to lull me into a false sense of security, and the police would return those clothes in their entirety as soon as they make the dumb Arab change into stripy robes. But the Arab is not that dumb. The Arab is in new clean clothes. Where should I hide that Instruction in the plastic bag? Ah, there is a roll of duct tape. Excellent — I'll stick it to my body. Passport in the name of Hamid Kulani. It's good that Sari, who was adjusting the passport, left my original name so there's less confusion. And the fact that I used to be Shafi and became Kulani — what can I do? So, I'll put my passport in my wallet and my wallet in my pocket. Then, sandals…" The sandals on his feet were his own, ragged ones that he'd came in from Shudjaia, but that was alright, he'd buy new ones at the airport. Actually, it had better not be sandals. Azat, Abu Avada's son who visited Germany, said they didn't wear those there, only boots. "I'm going to be very, very quiet, on tiptoe… right, the door isn't locked. There are no fences in a what-they-call-it… a kibbutz, and that's good."

Soon, he is in the neighbour's yard, and then in the next street. "Subhan Allah — it's two in the morning and the Jews are asleep like hens in a henhouse. But I can't relax; can't relax! Where is the exit from this damned kibbutz? In which direction should I run? Wait, someone's approaching. That's the last thing I need now. As it is known, even a hare can eat its own kid in strange lands. It's good that steps can be heard from afar at night."

Having turned into the first alley, Hamid found himself at a playground. Even in the pale glow of the streetlights, the slide was flickering with different colours. Hamid glanced at its hot-yellow plastic slope, and imagining that Muhammad and Ahdaf were sliding on it, he choked. He plonked his gaunt butt on the rocking horse on springs, and it seemed the entire world shook beneath him.

"What is that stone cube of half-human height next to the garden swing? Oh, that's a drinking fountain."

Only now, Hamid felt how dry his throat was from the heat, bitterness, uncertainty and fear he would be captured. Jumping over the playground in two big leaps, he arrived at the cube and saw there were two fountains with buttons on both sides. Not to be an ass between two bundles of hay and not to offend any of the fountains, he decided to drink from both — first from the right and then from the left... or vice versa? "The clock hand goes from left to right indeed. The clock hand goes from left to right, but we write from right to left. Then we'll start from the right one."

The flow was very weak and thin. Between drinking, Hamid stopped for breath several times. He moved to the left fountain, bent very close to the metal aperture and pressed the button with all his might. A strong flow of water shot up into his face. Who knew?

***

'So,' a police lieutenant, Haim Sariel asked David Levin, 'all quiet?'

'What commotion can there be in the Saad kibbutz?' the latter answered whilst getting out of the car. 'Well, except for the rockets from Gaza and the "Iron Dome?"'

At that, he remembered a stupid phrase from some performance he'd listened to as a kid in Moscow: 'All is quiet in Baghdad.' What performance was that? Ah, right, Aladdin and some lamp… or was it Ali Baba and the Forty Thieves? He remembered only how he was sitting on a sofa in a… they did not use the word 'salon,' but instead called it the 'big room.' And grandmother on father's side, granny Nata, a Russian noblewoman in a dense Jewish environment, called it the 'living room,' pronouncing it a little nasally. Granny Nata felt quite comfortable in that Jewish environment. It was she who insisted on giving her grandson the Jewish name, David. Consequently, it was she who pronounced the sacramental: 'We are lifting our arses and leaving for Israel' with aristocratic parlance. "Granny, granny, I wish you are healthy for another hundred and twenty years."

So, where was he in his reminiscences? Ah, right, a gramophone record, Aladdin or Ali Baba? He didn't remember. He only remembered the song, "Persian peaches and green tea." He recalled sitting on the sofa and... they lived on the ground floor, and therefore there was a treillage on the window. He even wrote a poem about it: "I have a treillage on my window that is made of sunny rays."

David returned to his senses. The air became light and blue. A little more and the "Fortress opposite Gaza" created in memory of the enthusiasts who'd built Kfar Darom, Beerot Itzhak, and Saad, that recently seemed to be black, would turn to white. And those cypresses would become green. And the first rays of the sun would be caught by their tops. And the heavenly window would open. And there would grow... that same treillage in the form of sunny rays.

***

"Where should I look for him? The departure lounge is too crowded. There are no direct flights to Stuttgart. How is Hamid planning to get there: via Istanbul, Zurich, via Vienna?" What an idiot Moshe was. In the morning, when he found out that his night guest had run away, he should have called the police, saying that an Arab from Gaza was going to Germany using a fake Israeli passport. Why did he believe him?

But what was that? That jasper over there at the entrance to the gate leading directly to the lounge fenced in with the glass wall where they pass customs checks and passport control. That was his, Moshe's stripy white shirt and his grey jeans… That was him!

Moshe dashed through the hall.

'Your ticket, please?' delicately enquired a graceful employee of the airport fit to be his granddaughter, and with today's pace of young people, even to be his great-granddaughter.

Moshe stumbled. Should he explain the situation? Should he say: 'There's an Arab from Gaza flying with a fake passport?' Should he slander the dead children and kind journalist from Stuttgart — and what if it was all a lie? You never know why he needed to get to Europe… "Seriously, what should I do now? Raise an alarm? Well, imagine if the one calling himself Hamid was telling the truth. But he would get lost in that Germany. An Israeli prison would be better. Better? To land in a cell with other Arabs, maybe even terrorists? Or he could even be handed over to Abu-Mazen to let the Arabs deal with him themselves. And they would deal with him, indeed. No, everything had been done right. But what should I do now?"

'Your ticket, please,' the girl repeated.

His pocket started singing Mozart's fortieth symphony.

Curiously enough, but in some situations when you try to solve a problem and then your phone starts ringing, there appears a faint, feeble, and sometimes even unrealistic hope that someone who might help you solve this problem is trying to get through to you. Just like now. Well, according to the display, it was his neighbour and the secretary of the settlement, Zeev. Could Zeev help him solve this problem? Maybe Moshe was mistaken and Zeev would say: 'The Arab that stayed with you went for a walk at night, got lost, came to me, and now is sitting here waiting for you.'

He pointed at his phone so the girl would excuse him for a minute and stepped aside.

'Listening.'

'Moshe, where are you? Are you alive?'

'Well, hello. Why, why would I not be alive? I decided to go to the Ben-Gurion on some business.'

'Are you at the airport? Baruch Hashem! And you don't know a thing?'

'What should I know?'

'Your house has been bombed!'

'What? When?!'

'Twenty minutes ago. They launched Grad and "The Dome" didn't manage to intercept it.'

Dumbfounded, Moshe jumped up from the bench. Zeev was not a person to joke like that, and, obviously, nobody else would joke like that.

'The house? This can't be true. Completely, right? Completely destroyed?'

'Well, not completely, but one-third of the house is down, and the rest…'

'Zeev, wait, my wife is calling, too. Thank you. I'll call you back. Hello? Hello?'

'Moshe! Moshe! Moshe!' Dwora was crying over the phone. 'Are you wounded? Are you in pain?'

***

"And here is Europe," Hamid smirked, piercing into a red stripe on the sheet. "Imagine I come to Shudjaia and Ali would come out… No, Ali is not going to come out from anywhere ever."

Yes, Ali, who was executed; shot as a so-called agent of Shin Bet would never come out from anywhere ever again. And there is no Shudjaia anymore either. A pile of wreckage and burnt corpses, including those of children, is that Shudjaia? Well, there is Muhtar. Right, Muhtar Sadik. Muhtar would come out and ask: 'So, how's Germany?' And Hamid would say to him: 'What about Germany? There are bedbugs in Germany!' Muhtar would choke on his favourite coffee... though... what coffee? Coffee is dragged through the contraband tunnels and the Egyptians - it's not like it used to be during those golden times when Mursi was reigning there - the Egyptians are destroying those tunnels, and coffee costs way too much now, like all things. But Muhtar would drink his coffee, anyway. He would sell his last pair of pants, but would find the money for coffee. So, he would take a sip of that golden, precious coffee of his with cardamom and say: 'How can that be? Bedbugs in Germany?'

Blood on the sheet. His blood. That means they got him. "I wonder where?"

It was itching near his ankle. There is probably a huge bump there. Hamid drew his foot closer. There was no swelling, but a little wound, so tiny, as if a tiny vampire did a job there.

Hamid put his feet on the floor and stretched. He looked around the room.

Yesterday, when exited the airport, he plonked himself on the back seat of a taxi and mumbled in English: 'To a hotel in the centre of the city; the cheapest one.'

'The cheapest is The Hamburg,' said the black-haired taxi driver whose appearance did not comply with the common stereotype of a tow-headed German... 'But it is still expensive: a standard room won't cost less than a hundred euros a night.'

Hamid was surprised by the fact this brunet European knew the prices in the local hotels and only later realised he was speaking Arabic to him. And when he realised he pronounced one phrase: 'Where from?'

'From Cairo,' the guy responded. 'And you're from Palestine?'

"He figured that out by my accent," Hamid discerned. "I could have figured an Egyptian out by the accent too"... But he couldn't do anything as he started feeling motion sickness. The darkness outside was making his eyes ache, and the weariness of the last days was devouring him with its dark carcass. He paid the driver as if in a dream, handed the money and his passport to the girl who was playing the role of concierge as if in a dream, took the key, and took the lift to the second floor.

And now he was fresh and, though bit by ticks, was standing at the window looking outside at the street of the German city, at the passers-by who didn't tremble in fear and didn't grab their children so they could run as fast and as far as they could when they heard the signal of the phone announcing that they'd received a text message. Besides, the SMS they did receive were sent by their relatives or acquaintances, by advertisers, by anyone, but not by the command unit of the hostile IDF that warned the peaceful population that at such hour and such a place there would be an attack.

Opposite the hotel there was a very long three-storey building where a banner was stretched between the second and the third floors with an inscription first in black letters FITNESS / WELLNESS / KURSE, then in red — STRONG, FIT + SEXY... nur fur Frauen, and then in black again as if written by hand — ZUMBA. Those words were followed by an image of a half-naked woman.

Turning his back to the window, Hamid cast a look round the room. "So, dear friend, this looks like your shelter now." There was no humming of drones, no ruins, no corpses, no SMS informing that one needed to run, giving no clue where, no sound of the departing Hamas missiles, no sound of the approaching Jewish missiles. It was a cosy hotel room. It was clean, very clean, though fairly shabby. The corners were chipped off. Well, it was obvious that it was one of the cheapest hotels in the centre of the city. However, on the other hand, however cheap it was, they should have enough money for refurbishment. And why is there a whole rectangle cut out in the toilet door ten centimetres from the floor? That was a mystery. For better ventilation? Is that right?

Was it even possible that he, under whose feet only three days ago glass shards and the wreckage of somebody's house, of somebody's cosiness, of somebody's life were crunching, could pay attention to such things? Yes, he could. He still could. He Could! And if he could, that meant that he was alive.

He felt hungry. Hamid put on his clothes and went to the corridor. No sooner had he approached the glass door leading to the staircase than the built-in ceiling lamps suddenly flickered on, lighting his way. Interesting. Hamid felt as if he was a village dumbass who'd found himself in the concrete jungle. "And that's a shame that the lift stops only between the floors. It's most irrational. Whatever level you go, you need to take the stairs to get to your room."

There were no people in the hall. The girl that was sitting at the "reception", overweight and tow-haired, smiled and said: 'Your breakfast is ready and waiting for you.'

'Breakfast?' Hamid repeated, bewildered.

'Your breakfast is included in the price of your accommodation,' the hotel employee pronounced and smiled again.

Hamid was lost for a few seconds. Breakfast was included in the price? He didn't remember anybody mentioning that the day before, though another girl was sitting at the computer then. And though he was almost sleepwalking, he remembered the other one: she was also plump, but dark-haired with big brown eyes. No, it didn't seem that she'd mentioned anything about breakfast… or maybe she did, but could it be that his sleep while he was walking was especially strong then? And then, what about halal? What could a faithful Muslim eat from whatever they served here?

The tow-headed damsel interpreted his confusion as the blankness of a provincial and came out from behind the counter. She was wearing a hotel uniform, which was somewhat unusual — a black dress with a white apron, a tie which was made of two red ribbons, a flat straw hat upon a narrow flouncy cap, white stockings, and low-heeled shoes. Obviously, it represented the traditional clothing of some paysan from the suburbs of Hamburg.

With a gesture, she offered him to sit at a table and then went to the kitchen and gave some orders there, and on her return gladly announced: 'You'll have your scrambled egg now.' After that, she returned to her counter.

"How does she know I love scrambled eggs? Well, I could eat scrambled eggs alright, I guess, there couldn't be anything forbidden," Hamid thought, following the girl's solid silhouette with his eyes.

In his turn, he came up to the machine, tried various types of coffee, and decided on espresso. Of course, coffee without cardamom wasn't real coffee, any Arab would tell you that, but what could he do with those Europeans? Again, Allah is great. "Think, when did you last have coffee, Hamid? I remember. Yesterday at Moshe's. And before that, one month ago." That meant he needed to replenish that lack of coffee urgently. Indeed, the best Arabic compliment sounded like that: 'You grind coffee every day.' So, was he, Hamid, an Arab after all, or not? And if so, then... then that amount was not enough for him. They would pour three drops to the bottom of a paper cup and think that it was enough?"

He began pressing the button on the machine again and again until his cup was two-thirds full. Then he sat down at the table and, sipping the drink that we would consider heavenly and he thought was a travesty of the divine, started looking around the hall. Despite the name of the hotel, there were only a couple of views of Hamburg itself, though all the walls were covered with pictures of ships, wharves and ports. Here and there, there were glass windows with little models of sailing ships, and a model of a big caravel in the display window.

To the right of the counter, where one could get various juices and a fruit salad, there was a map. Approaching it, Hamid realised at once that he wouldn't be able to find Stuttgart there. Stuttgart was far in the south, and browsing the map, he found himself in the foggy north of Germany, bordered by the cold Baltics. "Kiel… Rostock… and here is Hamburg. Of course, it's the largest port. That's where the wharves and sailing ships came from."

And what was that stall next to the door? There were colourful pamphlets on the top, cheat sheets on the topic of what to see in that wonderful city firstly, secondly, and then what to visit later. And what was below? Wow, below was just the right thing — newspapers! Various newspapers were published in Stuttgart. Now he would look through the lists of the editorial staff members and he would definitely find Herman Schroder ("Ulenspiegel") in one of them. And then — it would be a mere formality…

Newspaper after newspaper with processed material was thrown to the nearby armchair. There were all kinds of Hanses, Hugos, Alberts, and Wilhelms flickering before Hamid's eyes; there were a few Hermans, but none among them was Schroder, and although there were a couple of Schroders, none of them were Hermans. And of course, none of the editorial staff had a journalist with the pen name "Ulenspiegel."

He needed to smoke that problem over. How did he not stock up on cigarettes in Ben Gurion? Once, in Rafah, he bought his favourite Pall Mall in a dark blue packaging and it cost him five times the price — fifty shekels; he could have bought as many packs as he wanted at a normal price at the airport, but he was too distracted and kept turning around to check if the police were after him. And now - there - he had one last cigarette left, and soon he would have to spend his precious euros to buy a new pack.

Hamid left the hotel; fortunately, the glass sliding doors were open all day. Wow, metal ashtray boxes were hanging on the walls on both sides of those doors. One could smoke as much as one wanted.

Taking a sweet puff, Hamid suddenly remembered how he'd discovered for himself those cigarettes-toothpicks for the first time, how he'd enjoyed them sitting on a bench in the garden of the Al-Vafa Hospital, waiting for Latifa who worked as a nurse there to come out. And how all of a sudden that fat Yasser Tirawi from the opposite house approached him while he was sitting on that stone bench, glanced at him spitefully and

asked: 'Hal' anta nablusi? — Are you a Nablusian?'
For some reason, citizens of Nablus were traditional-
ly associated with homosexuals. And if you smoked
ladies' cigarettes, then you were a faggot. Since then,
Hamid hadn't once heard that question when lighting
his cigarette: "How long is it since you've last been to
Nablus?" A couple of times, he even gave way to his
temper and let them have it in the face. Hamid put out
the cigarette, carefully folded it, and placed it into the
wall ashtray. "Just look how clean their pavements are.
They're probably clean because people don't shit in the
streets. Not even speaking about Gaza, but even Israel
is far away from these Germans." Though he'd only
been to Israel in transit, but people said that.

"Oh, I wish it was as clean in our area," Hamid
thought. "But one's still gotta teach our people. It is
truly said — 'a wild goose never laid a tame egg.'"

This was a picture Hamid hadn't ever seen in his
life and could barely even imagine that it was possible. A ginger-haired lass passed him by on high heels
that increased her fair height by ten percent; she was
wearing jeans that were three sizes too small for what
they were tightly covering, so that the denim seemed
to be just a blue paint that covered her naked skin in a
thin layer. But this wasn't the most amusing thing. The
lady was leading a beautiful… cat on a leash. The cat

was snow white, exuberantly fluffy with pinkish ears and tender blue eyes. The owner seemed to be slender though tightly built, and the cat obviously suffered from excess weight, but both had an equally majestic swagger.

'Persian?' Hamid asked, hardly concealing his amazement. The woman nodded and, in her turn, asked him with a smile: 'Are you a cat-lover?'

Hamid shrugged his shoulders, and the couple moved on, having waited for an answer in vain.

Did he love cats? Not really. Back home in Gaza it wasn't a thing to keep a pet at home.

He had some dubious feelings towards them. On the one hand, it was known that the Prophet Muhammad, once, when he was going to prayer, found that his cat was sleeping on the bottom part of his clothes. At that moment, he was in a hurry for namaz and didn't want to wake the animal up. And what did God's messenger do? He cut out the part of his clothes where his beloved pet was sleeping. And the collection of hadiths of Bukhari tells a story about a woman who was thrown into Gehenna because she locked her cat up and starved it until it died of hunger. On the other hand, many Muslims consider cats as impure animals because they're predators, which means they can use as food something from najis (impurities), for example, the intestines of their victims. Therefore, the touch of a cat's tongue to water or a person is also considered impure.

He recognised a Persian in the white beauty because it was the spitting image of Sonya, the cat that belonged to that same Russian, Zakiya, whom he'd mentioned the other day to Moshe. When Sonechka got ill, Zakiya wrote to international organisations on pet protection, and told her story in the Russian-speaking group on Facebook "Israel loves cats." As a result, she managed to do the impossible — to transport Sonya to the representatives of the Israeli organisation on pet protection, Tnu la-haet lihyet via the security gatehouse, Erez. Sonya's state improved, but the veterinarians continued with their treatments and observation. Until the beginning of the war, Zakiya constantly kept in touch with the clinic.

By the way, many people in Shudjaia expressed their indignation at Zakiya's deed.

'Children are dying here in hospitals,' they hissed, 'and she's consumed with animals.'

'You are the animals!' Zakiya lashed back at them.

It often happens that you get stuck with some problem, and it seems there is no solution. Then you get suddenly distracted, and when you get back to the problem, you look at it with fresh eyes and see everything differently. And now, before Hamid managed to return to his distressing affairs, a new thought hatched: "Even if Schroder is not one of the editorial staff, he's still published in the newspapers. That's called freelancing." That meant he needed to look through the newspapers until he came across his name or his pseudonym not only among the editorial employees, but as someone signing the articles. And whatever newspaper he would find him in, then he would need to run to that editor's office. It couldn't be that they didn't have the phone number of their employee, even if he was a freelancer.

Hamid returned to the hall and dashed to the pile of newspapers desperately tossed aside at the armchair. Looking through one after another, he started scanning the signatures under articles. He didn't understand a single word of what was written there, but it wasn't important... Schroder Herman ("Ulenspiegel")... Schroder Herman ("Ulenspiegel")... Schroder Herman ("Ulenspiegel")... The corpses of the newspapers were falling one upon the other. Not understanding what was going on and not knowing what to do, Hamid decided to have another smoke break. He took the empty dark blue Pall Mall box from his pocket, crumpled it up, and went to the machine to buy a new pack.

There was no blue Pall Mall there, so Hamid decided to get a white Marlboro pack. It is commonly known that the white colour is the sign of "light" cigarettes. He put four and a half euros into the slot, but nothing came out of the machine. Hamid approached the girl at reception and complained about the greedy machine. It wasn't that blond girl anymore; it was that other, from the night, with brown eyes. The girl looked away from her computer, came out from behind the counter and floated past Hamid, swaying her hips and playing with some plastic card like a Visa in her hand. She either inserted it into some slot of the machine or just pressed it against the screen on the front side of it.

'That's it,' she gently said to Hamid. 'You can use it now.'

As she floated back to the counter, she bestowed an almost official smile on the Arab, also burning him with her eyes filled with such passion that Hamid felt uneasy: "What's wrong with her?"

Marlboro turned out to be yuck - nothing "light" about it at all. Having taken a few puffs, Hamid had to agree with the writing on the pack. Though he could not read it all, he understood the word '*Impotenz*' alright. It was clear what it would lead to in the doctors' opinion, and he glumly admitted: "Smoking these cigarettes definitely leads to that." Clearly, no bright ideas would come into one's head under the influence of these. While standing at the entrance, Hamid was staring vacantly when his eye caught a mat with the writing 'Herzlich Willkommen' on it. "Well, 'Willkommen' is probably related to the English, 'Welcome,' but what is 'Herzlich?' Ah, of course, 'Herr' in German is 'Mister,' everybody knows that. So, 'Herzlich Willkommen' is 'Welcome, ladies and gentlemen.'

Hamid was doubly happy, both for solving that unexpected puzzle so easily and that he'd managed to distract himself from the problem and he could have a fresh angle on it again. The fresh angle was useful indeed — in a second, Hamid, inspired by a new idea, stood at the reception glancing at the melting from desire plump girl and gnarling into the phone.

'Hello, is this an information desk? Information desk? Information desk?'

'Let me do it,' the fatty said mildly and at the same time imperatively, and literally grabbing the receiver from Hamid's hand, she started repeating at his dictation: 'Schroder Herman, ja, ja.'

Then there was silence — apparently, she was waiting for the answer. Suddenly, saying yet again another 'ja, ja,' she shrugged weirdly and began to jabber in German vehemently. Then silence ensued again, during which the girl eloquently rolled her eyes a couple of times, and then squinted them at Hamid as if asking, 'so, what do you think about me?' and then again 'ja, ja,' and having listened to the final verdict, she put down the receiver disconcertingly.

'There is no Herman Schroder in Stuttgart. There are a few other Schroders — Heinrich, Curt... but it's no use calling them. Schroder is a common last name. They are likely to be just people bearing the same family name.'

'And what if they are relatives and they know where...?' Hamid whispered.

'It's unlikely,' the girl replied, shrugging her shoulders. 'We will just lose time.'

'So, what are we going to do then?' Hamid mumbled, completely at a loss.

'Let's think... So, you say he's a journalist with the pseudonym "Ulenspiegel?" Ok. Take a seat over there for now, have some coffee and I'll browse the internet. By the way, my name is Marion.'

'Thank you, Marion,' Hamid muttered.

A few minutes later, she came up to Hamid and informed him: 'Herman Schroder, pseudonym "Ulenspiegel" is regularly published in the newspapers, *Stuttgarter Allgemeine Zeitung* and *Neue Stuttgart Zeitung* and also on the websites. The editor's office of *Neue Stuttgart Zeitung* isn't far from here — Schloßstraße 17, only... I think it would be better if... mmm... if we go there together.'

'Why?' Hamid asked.

'You see… as far as I understood, your Herman Schroder is a freelancer and is published in various newspapers.'

'And?'

'And that means that someone at the editor's office might give you his home phone or address or an email, or maybe not. And… it would be better if we go together.'

***

One-third of the house, but what a third! The floor was covered with chippings which until recently were part of the wall, and the other wall looked like a burnt skeleton from which the veins of wires like cobwebs loosely hung. Instead of the ceiling, there were just bare purloins. The bathroom door was torn apart, and inside there was a shower curtain hanging from the plastic rail like a dangling white flag sprinkled with whitewash. And here, there was no corner of the house at all — instead of it there were concrete blocks with wires jutting out of the carcass.

He walked around his house, and under his feet, stacks of boards and planks were springing and shards of glass were crunching through which he was looking at the trees, people, and the sky only yesterday. The

armchair was standing here, his favourite armchair...
but there were only charred flinders left now. Yesterday, he was sitting here remembering Shimon. And he
would have been sitting there today too, right at this
moment when the Grad hit, but for...

But for... but for...

And that was the "heder bitahon," the refuge
chamber. It had given way under the direct hit.

So that was what the cold sweat was. Moshe had
lived to the age of sixty and only now realised that cold
sweat when one looked at the spot where his corpse
should have lain. And it could have lain there, but
for... bur for...

But for Hamid!

***

Before going outside, Marion managed to change
her clothes. Instead of a stupid straw hat and all that
steeped in centuries uniform, she was wearing a trendy
dark grey jumpsuit with trousers flared from the hip,
and a bag of the same colour bag a long fringe hung on
a bare, chubby shoulder.

Filled with old but rather tall houses, the street
curved in an arch. Hamid and Marion went along the

tramlines. It was not far to go, although a couple of times they were still overtaken by a shiny new yellow tram. The century or two-century-old pseudo-Gothic edifices were suddenly replaced by quite modern cube-houses.

'We are here,' Marion announced and, having left Hamid in front of a heavy door squeezed in between massive display windows, went inside by herself.

'What about me?' Hamid asked.

'You wait here,' she replied, then looking critically at Hamid from head to toe once again, and equally critically shaking her head, she stated glumly: 'Arab.'

'But why? Why?' Hamid rebuked. 'So what if I am an Arab? Don't they sympathize with us? They love us, don't they?'

'At a distance,' stated Marion, and entering the building, she slammed the door right in front of Hamid's nose. Only slammed. She did not lock it, though…

…this cannot be! It's a delusion! This green door was an exact copy of the one to which he'd dashed back then, on that damned day, to save Muhammad and Ahdaf. There were drops of white paint that seemed to have appeared from nowhere in the upper right corner. And someone had scratched out the letter ال

"Tā' marbūṭa" below. And what was that? Where

did those red spots appear? Allah is great! Those were the imprints of his own hands when he was clenching with his scratched and bloody fingers to that locked door, the door to the entrance which was never locked before, and that had now become impenetrable. And he was trying so vehemently, unsuccessfully, and desperately to take it down, to break it down, to force it open. And then… and then there, in the east, there was the most horrendous sound growing at an insane speed. And then it hit! The earth shattered. And through that thunder, he could hear the choir of horror, and Hamid thought he could hear Muhammad and Ahdaf call for him in that tumult. And then silence again, and only the roar of collapsing purloins and the crackling of the growing fire. And then the abyss opened, from which oceans of fire poured out — first scarlet, then ginger, and then orange — and black smoke. And it was undying. He was standing in the middle of the street looking up, and stared and stared at that eruption, at that ginger, scarlet, black and golden lava… And he saw the Hamas commander with the short beard approaching the door without a mask. He took out a key from his pocket, slowly opened the door on which the first flakes of ash had already landed, and with a gesture, he ushered in Hamid heartily.

'There…'

Marion's voice brought him back to his senses. He looked around. The door was completely different. The drops of paint were not at all white, unlike those in Shudjaia, but light beige. And 'Tā' marbūṭa' was not 'Tā' marbūṭa' at all, it was just a scratch. There were no blood prints there at all — Hamid had imagined them.

Hamid looked under his feet. There were two cigarette butts, one smoked till the filter, and the other smoked to the middle. That meant it was him who'd smoked them while he was daydreaming. Admittedly, those nasty things could be smoked only in an unconscious state.

'And how long will you need to collect yourself?'

Looking at him scornfully, Marion gave a piece of paper to Hamid, who was trying to pull himself together, and who looked as if he was sleepy. He was slowly flowing from that universe where his children were burning alive to the one where the German lady was shaking him, standing on a quiet German street.

Almost mechanically, he took the small green square and saw a set of digits and the name of the person he was looking for.

'Freelancers,' Marion clarified, 'don't sit in the editor's offices. It's good that they gave me the phone number.'

'Then we should go to the hotel quickly,' Hamid blurted, suddenly inspired. 'I don't have a mobile phone. I'll call from your… well, from your counter… there's a phone there.'

'I have a phone here,' Marion said calmly, taking out and benevolently offering her cell phone from her purse with the fringe. 'You can call now.'

***

But Hamid didn't manage to make the call. First, there were boring beeps which lasted so long that Hamid started thinking that Schroder was going home from somewhere and heard, also from afar, his home phone was ringing and how he, Hamid was breathing into the phone, shaking with impatience, and Schroder was hurrying, hurrying. But he didn't manage to get it. The phone then clicked, and a pleasant woman's voice started neatly saying something in German. Grabbing the apparatus from Hamid's hands, Marion nervously pressed it to her ear and pronounced almost gleefully: 'The person you are calling is out of range. Please leave a message.'

"A message? What about? That he wanted to meet him? But how would they reach each other, then?"

'You must buy a cell phone for yourself. Have you got money?'

Hamid nodded.

'Well, that's good. Go straight along this street and you'll reach Königstraße. There's a shop, "Clove." I have to go; I still have to work until five. I could barely persuade Katrin to replace me for an hour.'

She turned around sharply and moved away.

'Thank you very much!' Hamid shouted at her back.

Marion stopped stone still.

'Thank you? Huh, no, you won't get away with just one "thank you." I'm finishing at five sharp, and at five sharp you'll be waiting for me in your room.'

'Waiting for what?'

The clicking of her heels was the only answer he received.

***

An elderly woman wrapped in a shawl was sitting on the pavement, rocking herself from side to side, and singing...

Coming closer, Hamid discovered that he was a slightly mistaken. First of all, she wasn't very old. Well, maybe around forty-fifty, but no more. That is, say, in the eyes of his father, let Allah rest his soul in peace! — she would be considered an old woman, but nowadays doctors worked so well... well, a forty-five-year-old woman was not old. But this woman looked so aged. Secondly, what did he mean by 'singing?' Howling — yes, wailing — yes, but singing? It could hardly be called singing. One couldn't even discern the words. Clearly, it was not an Arabic language. It was more likely to be Turkish, and maybe Farsi. But she was the only Muslim he met in Stuttgart in all that time, except for the night driver. And they say there are Muslims everywhere in Europe. So where were they? He'd been wandering around the city for an hour and hadn't seen a single one. No, there were quite a few dark-skinned people, but who knew where they were from? Maybe some Brazilians or Greeks? A Muslim must wear Muslim garments. Though in Gaza and even in his own Shudjaia, there were plenty of Muslims who wore foreign clothes. But that was at home, and one should enhance his faithfulness to Allah living among infidels. Of course, he was wearing European clothes, if not to say – Jewish... well no, there was nothing Jewish in these garments, only the fact that they were passed on to him by a Jewish guy. That was it, though. Was it his fault that half of his jellabiya, all in shreds was left in the tunnel between Beit Hanoun and Kissufim? As soon as he took a look around, he would buy some national clothing for himself, for sure. But now, he had a more serious problem — hunger and how to deal with it in a country where pork was the national dish.

Having called Schroder from the newly purchased phone yet again, and having listened to the monologue of the answering machine, he came up to the singing old woman, squatted, and asked her politely: 'Hal' umkynuka an tansahuni ila mat"am halal? — Can you recommend a halal restaurant?' Based on how the woman staggered back, he realised that she didn't understand Arabic.

Five minutes later, after the fiasco with the old Turkish or Persian woman, Hamid recognised his own in some bearded teenager, but he approached him with a certain wariness — in Gaza, such an appearance would distinctly indicate belonging to Hamas.

'A restaurant?' the young, bearded man gestured. 'Go straight, and in five minutes there will be shawarma.'

And in five minutes, he was home again. He sat at a table, ate authentic shawarma and drank real coffee with cardamom. Hamid closed his eyes. The smells... the smells were those from home, his very own. And the speech... the speech was Arabic, though with some unclear accent which sounded like Tunisian. There were screaming children running around the chairs... and if he closed his eyes tightly, he could imagine they were Muhammad and Ahdaf.

'So, have you looked around yet? How is it in The Hamburg?'

Hamid opened his eyes and blankly stared at a man in a black t-shirt who was shaking him by his shoulder.

'Don't you recognise me? Right, you were falling asleep all the way then. I'm Gamal, the driver who brought you to the hotel from the airport yesterday.'

***

'You're asking what grief made me leave Gaza, willed by Allah, and move to your cold Germany? So, Gamal, listen. I used to live in Shudjaia, a suburb of Gaza, I prayed to Allah, worked at a school, and taught English to the children. They say here in Germany it's forbidden to hit children with a whip. And believe it or not, for the twelve years that I worked at the school, I never once hit anybody. I was even summoned to the principal's office once — he said that the discipline in my class suffered and I was too liberal with those bastards.'

'People say,' Gamal, who was half-dozing, interrupted, opening one eye, 'it's better to make a child cry than cry later about him. And do you have a wife?'

'I had one,' Hamid replied. 'She was beautiful…
her name was Aya.'

'Just one?'

'I didn't need a second one. And we had three
sons — Mamduh, Ahdaf, and Muhammad. We didn't
have our own house. Well, for the last nine years we
had a siege, so it was impossible to find building mate-
rials as everything goes towards building bunkers and
tunnels, and even if you find something, then it costs
crazy money. I guess we were possessed when we chose
Hamas for ourselves.'

'You probably voted for them in the election?'

'Of course, but everyone was voting for them.
It seemed so easy: Fatah was full of thieves, and Hamas were honest, faithful people who were, by the way,
gathering a lot of donations for the poor; Fatah lost intifada and Hamas won. The Jewish army enters Ramallah and Shkhem where Abbas rules as if they were coming home, and they shoot and arrest anyone they want,
and they extract the army and forcefully ban settlers
from Gaza where the Hamas warriors shoot Qassam
rockets. In my head, I understood there was nothing to
be joyful about, but we didn't see anything bad in the
Jewish greenhouses in their settlements and from the
construction in the settlements themselves; we didn't
see anything bad, only workplaces what with our wide-

spread unemployment. And the main thing — it was clear to me that the occupation is definitely bad, but the bandits in the government like ours, as in Ramallah, were even worse.

'I understood that, but when there was exultation in the streets where pupils ran with sherbet and muhallebi and congratulated you, and when your wife came home from work beaming with happiness, then like it or not, you became infected with this mood and your feet started dancing by themselves. And then, there were elections coming up. And then, when the euphoria died down, we realised who we had chosen, but not at once. Besides, with time we understood something more — those black days of occupation when one could speak whatever he wanted, had passed, and now we needed to keep our mouths tightly shut if we didn't want to utterly disappear like Ali Suef, who expressed his regret that back in 2003 the Israelis only wounded Ismail Haniyeh when they shot him from the air.

'But life went on. Sons were being born, pupils were growing up, and the grey-haired people whom Aya treated were getting better. Unfortunately, on the day Hamas soldiers were shooting from the territory of the hospital where Aya worked, Mamduh came to see his mum. And he did. Then I saw their scorched corpses — they were lying at the fence of the hospital garden. They were struck by a response hit from Israel... Do you know what it is to bury your child? Do you know what it is to turn away, biting your lip, when your children ask: "Daddy, when will mum and Mamduh return?"

'Day after day, the Jews attacked Shudjaia. Day after day, Hamas's people shot from the yards, schools and houses, and the Jews were complacently responding to them, destroying missile launching sites abandoned by the bandits and killing peaceful people Hamas was using as human shields. I was astounded by both parties. Why would the Jews set themselves up? Couldn't they do something else and not play the scoundrels game? And I was surprised by Hamas, too. Alright, those indifferent reporters who were just listing how many missiles fell on the territory of Israel like a tongue twister focused their cameras on the ruins from which pieces of carcasses stuck out, on the gory bodies, and at the children with tied-up stumps instead of arms and legs. I mean, there should be a journalist, I thought, who, like Ulenspiegel, would admit the ashes of Shudjaia into his heart? Wh-what? Ah, who Ulenspiegel is? Well, it's the main character of a novel by a Belgian writer who... ah, well, it doesn't matter.

'What's important is that sooner or later, there would appear such a journalist, and he would shout

out to the entire world that the king is naked and would tell the whole world who the genuine perpetrator of our pain, our blood, and our ashes is. But the journalist didn't appear, and our houses kept on being destroyed… And then, one day, I received an SMS where the Israeli were warning me that my house was in the engagement area, and they requested that we leave immediately. Muhammad, Ahdaf and I jumped as we were straight into our jalopy Fiat and headed for the hills and far away. Ah, if only I'd chosen the hills in the other direction, maybe my children would still be alive. We didn't get too far — a couple of blocks, maybe three, and then the street was blocked there. They dragged us out of the car, forced us into that four-storey house, and made us go upstairs. And then, there was the roof.'

***

The car turned left and dove under the bridge and dashed along the main avenue of Pardes Hanna, now and then slowing down at *kikar* — small round square crossroads.

"Dwora was right. Indeed, after the South, which didn't have breaks from bombing, the silence was bewildering. The silence was written on people's faces."

What was he thinking about? The main thing was to assess what had happened to him. So, the moment he was sitting in his car at the gas station, an Arab came up to him and asked where he, Moshe, was going. Was it a casual occurrence? Of course, pure coincidence. As a result, the Arab came to his house — that was a coincidence too, but not so… pure, so to say. Though, on the other hand, could he call it dirty or what? It was just normal when you meet a person who has nowhere to go to offer him to share your bread and your shelter. This is what the Almighty demands from us. Yes ,yes, that same one Moshe was so ardently praying to on the shore a few minutes before that weird occurrence. That means there was nothing accidental in the fact he gave refuge to the wanderer. Moving on. At night, the guest disappears. Ok, Arabs' behaviour is completely unpredictable. That is, let's call it a coincidence, though, truth be told, there is some logic in it, only we don't see it.

Having noticed the Arab was missing, Moshe found himself facing a choice — whether to call the police, start the "chase" by himself, or just let it go. Was he a warden to this brother of his, a cousin? The last option wasn't good, because yes, he was a warden. He, Moshe, just like other people, was a descendant of Seth, and not Cain, to answer like that. And it looked like everyone was responsible for each other. But the first solution wasn't an option either. He thought about it not once — it meant he would frame up Hamid, maybe even risk his life. Therefore, there was no choice, no real choice for Moshe. He could not, he could not not go to the airport. And it meant there were no accidents in that chain of "coincidences." That means that Hamid was sent to him by the Almighty in order to save Moshe, and not just that Moshe was sent by the Almighty to save Hamid.

"Wow, stop it, not so fast!"

Having said to himself all that, Moshe automatically pressed the brakes, which caused a long honk from a Mazda which almost hit his fender, and which was followed by the best wishes of its owner.

Moshe pulled his Subaru over closer to the pavement, manoeuvring with his saved fender and let the Mazda overtake him, whose owner turned out to be a charming blond, who was paying more attention to her reflection in the rear-view mirror, admiring her beauty, than to the road.

"But he really saved me, and I... I don't even know where he is now," Moshe concluded with chagrin as he drove into the courtyard of the house where one of his daughters lived and where now his Dwora was conquering the heights of pedagogy, grazing her grandchildren. Numerous multi-coloured cats, usually residing on the local garbage dump, fluttered out from almost under the wheels. It stank of cigarettes again. Why was this smell haunting him when there wasn't even anyone around?

Moshe went up the stairs and pressed on the doorknob. The next moment, he was hugged by Dwora with babies hanging from her. The most dexterous ones — five-year-old Haim and six-year-old Meir, managed to crawl from grandmother to grandfather and now swayed on him as if from a liana.

After a vivacious greeting, Moshe, having left the bags at the door, headed for the room allotted to him and Dwora. In fact, compared to how Moshe's numerous offspring who left the bombarded South all crowded into Leia's apartment, the infamous herrings in a barrel could just halloo each other in all that space.

Once finally alone, Moshe ran to the computer. Whilst it was loading, he impatiently snapped his fingers. Finally, the long-awaited 'Google' appeared on his screen. Moshe quickly moved his fingers over the keyboard and in the search bar there appeared: "Herman Schroder (Ulenspiegel)."

***

'In general, as they say, you are running away from the rain and get caught in the torrent. What to do then? I went on the off chance, and can you imagine, a bit later I heard… you know, some hissing and rustling. I mean, it was far away, a few kilometres away from Saad; it was the night highway breathing. The highway never freezes, never sleeps. The highway was waiting for me, the highway was striving to help me, the highway, when I finally reached it, avoiding the security guards of the kibbutz in the dark, sent me a taxi with a driver, a real Jew who immediately understood I was an Arab, but he didn't care at all, he was only interested in the money. He was ready to sell his Jewish mother for money; I told him I needed to get to Ben Gurion Airport, and he drove me and the kind highway carried me away from the Jews, away from the Arabs, to the only person in the world who wasn't indifferent to the bloodshed of my children, to Herman Schroder, Ulenspiegel… And the main thing I'm taking with me…'

He wanted to say about the Instruction, but suddenly fell silent.

Gamal carried on sitting with his eyes closed.

"Has he fallen asleep while listening to me?" Hamid wondered.

'Gamal,' Hamid whispered.

'I'm thinking, thinking, I'm not asleep!' Gamal responded irritably.

'Thinking?' Hamid asked at a loss. 'What are you thinking about?'

'I am thinking about whether you're hopeless or not.'

'Me? What do you mean, hopeless?'

Hamid didn't understand a thing, and Gamal, without opening his eyes, continued reasoning as if not hearing him, and maybe, actually, not hearing him at all.

'Suppose one can persuade or buy you? It means that you're not hopeless. The other option is that one can neither persuade you nor buy you. It means that you are hopeless, and then you need to be killed.'

'Me?' Hamid asked again, not even terrified but more surprised.

'Well, definitely not Schroder," Gamal sighed, tiring of communicating with such a thick person. There was some amazing firmness in his voice, where in those moments where exclamations were supposed to sound, there was only calmness. 'There is nothing to kill Schroder for yet. But if you supply him with unadvisable material, then we'll have to get him, too. And in order for it not to happen, preventively, it will be just you.'

'I mean, if you're not going to kill me, then you'll be persuading me. But of what?'

'Of this!' Gamal shook and perked up. He wasn't lying back in his chair and dosing anymore, but was nervously lighting a cigarette from the butt of another. 'Enemies invaded our land. Enemies sent hundreds of thousands of our people into exile. Only with their existence and their attempt to establish their own power on the territory of Islam, they offend our faith.'

'Wait, wait, Gamal, you are an Egyptian, not a Palestinian! Where does that Hamas bullshi… these Hamas ideas come from? Are you one of the "brothers-Muslims" by any chance?'

'We are all brothers, and all Muslims,' Gamal replied evasively. 'And we're still gonna get that bastard, As-Sisi. But for him, I wouldn't be stuck here with you in Stuttgart for a damn… I'd be walking the streets of Cairo instead.'

"Hamas guys, brothers-Muslims," Hamid thought. "What the hell is the difference? As they say, onion always smells the same."

'Our enemies have got tanks, planes, and that damned "Dome," Gamal continued, 'and what have we got? Almost nothing. Grads that they hit like apples from the trees, Kalashnikovs with which our guys are trying, without any success, to crawl out from the tunnels on the territory occupied by the enemy, cornetcy and RPGs with which they greet the hostile vanguard from the ruins of their houses. We are practically defenceless. And with that, we still win. We win all the time. We threw them out from Gaza. We threw them out of Lebanon. We sabotaged their attempts to overthrow Hamas' rule in Gaza. We have a powerful weapon — our pain… Just look!'

He passed Hamid a piece of paper folded into four.

'What's that?'

'These are extracts of the instructions from the Ministry of National Defense, and not Hamas, but your beloved Abu-Mazen. The instructions for the media and bloggers. Just read it.'

'Any deceased person should be first of all be called a "civilian," Hamid started reading, 'and only then can you mention his status in the jihad or military rank. Do not forget to always add "an innocent citizen" or "a civilian" to the name of the deceased.

'Start your reports on attacks by the Palestinian opposition with the phrase: "In response to the cruel Israeli aggression," and finish it with the phrase: "Such-

and-such number of people have died since the beginning of the Israeli aggression in Gaza". Always follow the formula "the attack is in response to the occupation -Palestinians only react."

Follow the reports of Israeli representatives. Always discredit them, defy them, and present them as a lie.

Avoid the publications of photographs of missiles launched into Israel from the residential districts of Gaza. Do not publish photographs of places where the fire is on.

Do not publish photographs of our soldiers in masks and with heavy weaponry so that we are not accused of instigating violence.

When communicating with Western journalists, use rational political language and avoid emotional outbursts. Our goal is to expose the villainy of occupation and condemn it as violence.

Do not try to persuade Western people that the Holocaust was a lie. Do not deny the Catastrophe. On the contrary, use it for comparison to show that right now, Israel is doing the same thing to the Palestinians.

Use the narrative of life against the narrative of blood. When you are talking to Arabs, speak of the deceased as martyrs who fell in actions with the aggressors, but when you are talking to the Western people, speak of the deceased as peaceful citizens. Speak about the huge number of the wounded. Show the human face of the Palestinian sufferings. Vividly describe ordeals of the peaceful residents under the oppression of occupation and bombings.

Do not publish photographs of military commanders. Do not mention their names and do not praise their successes during conversations with foreign friends.'

"What an interesting instruction," Hamid thought. "And it wonderfully intertwines with that other instruction that is attached to my body with scotch tape under my shirt."

'There, my dear,' Gamal continued. 'That is, do not stand up against your people. Anyway, you won't be successful in doing so. All the same, the Jews will lose. Idiots! They thought that the "Iron Dome" was their salvation, but it's actually their downfall. With that "Dome" we'll attain that state when stupid Christians and other pagans who don't think much of Jews which will make them get lost from our land.'

'Why?' Hamid was confused.

'Because, you dumb-head, earlier, at least once in a while, a random missile would get into a Jewish house and they, in response to our generously demonstrated blood rivers - sometimes actually it was just red paint - they, being somewhat confused and as if apologising, would provide some corpse to the world. And now, we are writing notes and they are playing. We are launching a missile and they, naturally, hit it; we launch again, and they hit it again, too. And that happens until they lose patience, and that's when they start firing at us in response. And the main thing then would be to leave under that fire the maximum number of innocent victims. So that the screens all over the world are filled with the dead faces of our babies, murdered at the hands of the bloodthirsty Jews, and the crying mothers throwing their hands up to Allah, their faces distorted with grief. So that all people in all corners of the world will clench their fists with hatred. So that lips will whisper by themselves: "Hitler was right." So that the entire world will say: "Occupiers, leave the Palestinian lands." So that, being wary of the people's wrath, the politicians will vote for the creation of the Arab state and the demolition of the Jewish…

'I mean… you've gone too fa-a-ar,' Hamid murmured wistfully, without returning the sheet to Gamal. 'I don't think any nation would unseat their ruler just because he supports Israel.'

'Look at these people,' Gamal uttered, waving his hand.

Hamid raised his eyes unwillingly. There were

tall, blonde and dark-haired men and women around, some of them passing by the café chatting about something or hurrying on their business, others sitting at the tables set on the pavement. Some of them were eating shawarma, some eating ice cream, some drinking coffee, and others beer.

'Look at these people,' Gamal repeated. 'They grew up feeling guilty before the Jews. Since the earliest age, the idea was drilled into their heads that hating Jews is a crime. But they are the descendants of those people who hated the Jews and had been destroying them for centuries, and, during one relatively recent decade, they were doing it with a peculiar passion. They are the bearers of the same genes of hatred.'

'Are you talking about Germans?' Hamid asked.

'It's about all Europeans. Even during the Second World War, other nations in Europe were also working hard in that field, some of them more than others. And that bigotry towards Jews didn't dissolve, it's just the aftershock raised by the results of that bigotry that made it into the unconscious. And now, oh, rejoice! — one can hate Jews and curse them out loud, publicly wish they were dead and not be considered an anti-Semite, and not even admit to oneself that they are anti-Semites. And there are those, which is like music to their ears, those Jews that actively participate in the anti-Israeli movement. Do you remember that retard who lived through Auschwitz and was going to help you as a passenger of the "Free Gaza" fleet? Just imagine, a Jew, a victim of Oswiecim, who fights against Israel. What kind of anti-Semites are we after that? We are anti-fascists. Now think, this hatred made millions, tens of millions of people join the front in the Second World War for perdition — won't it be able to demolish some Merkel if she dares to just squeak in support of that horrid, Nazi, hate-crazed Israel? And our task is to feed that bigotry so that it grows and bursts. And the firewood for this hatred is the bodies of our people — our men, women and children.'

'I mean… why children?' Hamid felt that his eyes were welling up with tears. "Damn! The last thing I need is to cry in front of this bastard." And the thought that he almost mentioned the Hamas Instruction when he was reading the Abu-Mazen instruction gave Hamid the shudders. He sipped his coffee, coughed, and repeated: 'Why children? Let those Hamas people be the firewood themselves.'

'And who will fight then? Who'll attack? We don't have children and adults – they're all soldiers. The entire nation is the army now. Do you understand? Commanders in the army don't throw themselves in the path of bullets — they send their soldiers to perish.

This is normal. Name me one army which is structured differently.'

Hamid felt Moshe's dry hand on his shoulder.

'IDF,' he said quietly, automatically putting the folded in four sheet into his pocket.

'What?' Gamal blurted.

'IDF,' Hamid repeated. 'There is no order of "Forward" in the IDF. There is an order of "Follow me."'

Gamal jumped up, his face turning a deep red — where did his tranquillity go? He grabbed Hamid roughly by the collar and hissed: 'You say the IDF? We'll show you the IDF, you wretch! Get this Satan out of Germany and forget about all those Schroder-Ulenspiegels, otherwise, you won't live!'

Hamid had never been known for having any particular strength, but here Gamal toppled over the table, breaking all the flimsy chairs on his way — obviously, all the grief of the last few weeks had been transferred into the power of Hamid's fist.

***

The tow-haired woman was at the reception.

'Where is Marion?' Hamid asked.

She squinted at him somewhat strangely and didn't reply. Hamid shrugged his shoulders and entered the lift. On reaching his floor, he approached his door when the door opposite his room opened. Unlike the other doors, there was no room number on it. A scrawny guy wearing glasses and a light white jacket came out, passing him by and enveloping him in the odour of a freshly smoked cigarette. And then Hamid realised what he wanted so much to do — to smoke. Since he'd hit Gamal and been barred from the café in shame with the words: 'You should thank us that we're not calling the police, otherwise, you, snake, you'd be wiggling in the cops' hands,' Hamid had been in a stupor and now realised that a cigarette, even a shitty one, would help him shake it off. Only, it seemed it was forbidden to smoke in the rooms - at least he couldn't find an ashtray in there. Truth be told, despite his passion for tobacco, Hamid didn't like to stay in smoke-filled premises. Don't smoke where you live and don't live where you smoke.

Should he really go downstairs again and out into the street? Wait, wait, and why did that young German leaving the room without a number on the door stink of smoke? Hamid went to the door of that strange room and carefully opened it slightly. There was no bed in the room, but there were two tables, a few chairs, and numerous filing cabinets and closets. There were bed sheets on the tables and folded woollen blankets on the chairs. It was some sort of utility room or a combat station of a chatelaine. The only unclear thing was what that scrawny pointy head was doing there — he didn't look like a chatelaine at all. Then Hamid noticed that right across from the entrance, instead of a window like in his room, there was a door that led to a balcony. He approached it and pressed the door handle. The door gave way, but Hamid didn't see a balcony but a metal staircase, circular, but with right angles. Apparently, it connected all the fire exits from every floor and then led outside, though they hadn't indicated that fact on the door of the room. Apparently, in case of a fire, the hotel guests were to guess for themselves that it was their way to salvation while running around in the fire and smoke. But it didn't matter. The main thing was that in a corner of the metal platform there was a plastic stool, and on it was an iron ashtray filled with cigarette butts. Hamid sat down, and, placing the ashtray on his lap, took out a cigarette and, almost without repulsion, sucked it down in a few puffs. He almost physically felt how everything inside settled down, how his nerves came to order, how something that lay like a black carcass on his soul transformed into a thundercloud, then a cloudlet, then a light cloudlet, and then dissipated, dissipated, dissipated. Having smoked his cigarette to the filter, Hamid moved back towards his room with a sense of accomplishment.

He stopped dead at the door. There was an inexplicable sense that there was someone in his room. Inexplicable because there was no rustle coming from there, and there was no streak of light visible from under the door. But with his sixth sense, he felt in his gut that there was someone inside.

Hamid remembered an American film he'd watched on TV several months previously. A mafia boss entered a bar, and there was an ambush. The undercover policemen were acting naturally — one smoking, one drawing on a whiskey soda, one was chatting with a friend that was his partner. But the bandit felt in his bones — cops — and dashed to the door. Hamid desperately wanted to dash too; he even stepped back a little, but then stopped. Not only because it seemed nonsense - well, who could it be there? – but mainly because he had nowhere to run.

He determinedly took his key with the long plastic number plate and, without further hesitation, placed it in the keyhole and pressed the door handle.

'And how long, I beg to ask, am I supposed to wait for you?' asked Marion. 'You were told to be here at five, and now it's half-past five. Are all guys from Gaza like this?'

'I mean… I didn't know…' Hamid mumbled.

'What didn't you know?' Marion snapped. 'That I spent my precious time on you and that you'd need to spend your time on me now? You know, tit for tat? And that didn't even occur to you? Shame on you!'

Hamid stood as if he was rooted to the floor.

'Why are you standing there like a pole?' Marion purred with the voice of an angel. 'Close the door and come here. Or have you completely forgotten under the bombs there how a man is different from a woman?'

Her hair was like a black waterfall cascading down her shoulders. Hamid leaned into it with his lips as if it was pure water flowing on a hot Palestinian day. She was stroking his short hair, and he felt as if he was a little boy in the comforting hands of his mother. Tears were running down his face. Never to become a grown-up, never to hear bombs exploding, never to see the blood flowing, never to…

**

The clip-clopping of Marion's heels were tailing off in the corridor, and with them that feeling of love which had awakened in him during the embrace tailed off too. Marion wasn't a mother, a resurrected Aya or a lifesaver Allah had thrown him from heaven. Lying in the bed, which still preserved the warmth of her body, he ruminated about why she, especially if she happened to lie on these sheets which she had given out herself - and he did not doubt that things like that happened with some regularity – didn't take care of preventing those six-legged vampires from crawling on those sheets. Or she did not suffer from them at all? Could it be that German girls were so tough-skinned? And then, if it was inconvenient for one person to lie on such a sunken mattress, when there were two people, then the poor thing on the lower level must be touching the floor with their butt. Couldn't she take some initiative and replace the mattresses?

With these deep thoughts, Hamid got up, put on his shirt and pants, and looked out the window. Salam Alaikum! What on Earth was that?

A yellow Peugeot briskly sped out around the corner and, passing by the hotel, stopped near that café, some fifty meters from the entrance. Four men hurtled out of the car and crossed the road, and one of them — the one who came out from the left front door, the driver was pointing at the hotel and explaining something to his companions, three black-haired guys in identical t-shirts, and, judging by their appearance, brothers in faith, or even Hamid's compatriots. Then he entered the café, and the other four moved towards the entrance of the hotel. Those few seconds that Hamid saw the driver were enough to identify unmistakably that it was Gamal.

'I wonder if they're looking for me?' he asked himself and answered at once. 'Of course, who else? He got it in his face and now wants to become even more closely acquainted.'

An Israeli missile missed Hamid in Gaza. Hamas' rockets didn't get him in Israel. And now, here in Germany… Out of the frying pan, into the fire. Just like during the Palestinian winter, icy trickles ran down his shirt, only now it was the icy sweat of fear.

Grabbing his passport, the Instruction, and a pack of money from the table, Hamid ran into the corridor. No, he couldn't use the usual stairs for his escape; they'd be using them to come up now. The light on the plastic doors of the lift also showed there were people coming upstairs between the second and the third floor. It looked like the dear guests divided into two groups intending to cut off all the getaway routes for him. Having stepped back into the corridor, Hamid almost automatically pushed the door of the room that was used as a utility closet. Hurrying inside, he slammed the door, jumped out to the metal fire stair escape, and dashed down three steps at a time. The last one was already in the front garden near a house, snuggling up at the back of the hotel. There was a bald, fair-bearded German sitting on the terrace drinking coffee. He glanced at Hamid in surprise. The latter pressed his finger to his lips, made his eyes look scary, drew his thumb across his throat, meaning — "if you turn me in, I'm going to cut your throat," and rushed deep into the yard with all his might, jumping over low fences and praying to Allah that it was a pass-through yard. Luckily, it was.

***

Hamid awoke to a hard blow on his side. A kick, to be exact, with a sharp boot tip. He opened his eyes. Two men were standing above him.

'Well, well, son of a swine, get up if you're a real

man. Get up and get what you deserve.'

The voice of the first scoundrel was high-pitched, almost shrill. Though he was clearly trying to speak calmly, one could feel that everything was boiling with indignation inside him.

'What kind of man is he?' the other one joined in. 'All he knows is to offer his ass to the Jews. Basically, he's a nablusi!'

"I could probably try to deal with these two with the help of Allah," Hamid thought. "At best, it would be a fight, not an ass-kicking."

He made an attempt to jump to his feet, and taking a full force blow to the face at once, tumbled down back onto the ground.

"Now there will be more blows," Hamid thought in dismay, and tightly closed his eyes.

However, there was no more beating. When Hamid finally opened his eyes, he discovered that he was still lying on a lawn near the Concert Hall, where'd he crawled out in the middle of the night from a pedestrian tunnel some three metres away so that he could sleep in the fresh air. There was nobody around. Was all that just a nightmare? It looked like it. Though his side was sore, there was a physical explanation to that in the form a sharp stone jutting from the ground which had obviously scratched him when he clumsily turned in his sleep. Nonetheless, the feeling of vulnerability did not leave the Arab, and, turning a little more on the grass, he went back to the same pedestrian tunnel which he'd left about four hours before. Even if the floor was concrete, it wasn't so scary.

***

There were repairs being done on the tramways on Schloßstraße. The asphalt was torn out like a fishes' belly, and the rails were shimmering in the rays of the morning sun.

"When will they finish those refurbishments?" Marion swore in her head. "When will I be able to use my close and favourite parking lot and not drag myself to the other end of the world on Silberburgstraße?" Suddenly, she felt that someone was watching her from behind the main entrance, where she was supposed to pass. And she was right; she noticed someone's nose there. Could it be bandits?

Marion looked around. The street was almost empty. There, near the Jewish Cultural Centre, some lonely elderly woman loomed in the distance.

"Those Russian freeloaders come in big numbers here. Now we have to provide them with housing because their grandfathers and grandmothers were exterminated by gas. But how would that old bag help her? Where is she? Where is that old woman? And even if she was closer, what could she possibly do? Those old women aren't trained to catch criminals; even the Russian-Jewish ones."

Marion stopped. She was afraid to go on. "Damnation take those roadworks! Now I need to drag myself through the middle of nowhere being watched by some suspicious type. I wish a policeman would appear from somewhere…"

And indeed, someone did appear, though it was not a policeman, but the owner of that nose who had caused the distress. Immediately, tranquillity spread in her soul and her plump and stout body — for the bearer of the nose turned out to be that country bumpkin from Israel or Palestine or, well, somewhere there, who had first tired her out with the search for that Stuttgart freelancer and then in bed, as if trying to pay her for her efforts, but being careful not to overpay by a single cent, and finally ran away in an unknown direction after those knuckle-draggers came after him. What can you tell me, dark-skinned nitpicker?

The Arab looked like nothing on Earth — he had dark circles under his eyes after a sleepless night, dark bristles on his face, and his shirt was as if he had worn it yesterday, then someone had washed the floors with it, dried it without even rinsing it and made him put it back on. The main thing was the fear that was frozen in his eyes. Pressing a finger to his lips — and in the empty street — he suggested with a sign to her to stand closer to the wall and started whispering ardently:

'Marion, I need shelter! Do you hear me, Marion? I'm being hunted! Do you hear me, Marion? They want to kill me! Help me!'

'I don't understand a thing,' Marion mumbled. 'Who's hunting you? Why?'

'I mean, they're afraid that I'm going to meet Ulenspiegel. They wanted to win me over to their side.'

'Who are they?'

'I mean, Arabs that live in Stuttgart. They came to kill me. I ran away. I managed to grab my passport and money and ran down the fire escape. I was wandering around the city until three in the morning, and at three I tried to get back to the hotel, but I noticed the dear guests who were watching the hotel entrance from afar, and I ran off.'

'What about a fire escape?' Marion stammered.

'Right. Do you think after realising I used it to run away, they won't keep an eye on that too? Of course, they will. Just you wait.'

'So, where did you go?'

'Where? Where? As I was, in a shirt and jeans, with my money, passport, and the Instr… Well, with my money and my passport in my pocket, I went wherever the road took me. I wandered and wandered for the rest of the night, dragging myself along some shady and empty alleys, and in the morning I asked the first person I met where a hotel was. He had no clue. I asked another one, and in the end a policeman explained everything to me; and he didn't forget to check my documents, of course. He was quite suspicious that a foreign guest was walking around so lightly dressed.'

'Did he directly ask you that?'

'He did…'

'And what did you reply?'

'That I left my suitcase at my friend's. And he said: "And why didn't your friend host you at his place?"'

'Why didn't you tell him that someone was chasing you?'

'I mean… what should I tell him? That I beat up a local Egypt-born citizen as soon as I arrived in Stuttgart? That I jumped off the balcony because four Arabs came up to the hotel? Would he believe me? And even if he did, do these policemen really need conflicts to do with Muslims here in their streets? Why the hell would he help me? I came, and the problems started. I mean, if there is no me — there won't be any problems.'

'Are you afraid the police will kill you?'

'I doubt they would kill me, but they would deport me using some excuse.'

'Alright, what's next then?'

'Next? He gave me the address of a hotel.'

'Which one?'

'Mercure Stuttgart.'

'Is it the one on Heilbronner Straße?'

'Yep. Heilbronner Straße 88.'

'And what's there?'

'How do I know?'

'Haven't you been there?'

'I mean… I have… I got there, shaking with exhaustion; I got the key, fell on the bed, and collapsed. I woke up as if I'd just emerged from the Dead Sea — my wife and I travelled there while there were Israelis, before the Oslo Accords. So, as if I came out from the Dead Sea, it seemed like I was on the shore already, but it felt like the water wasn't dripping down my body but crawling as if it was hummus or tahini. And the doziness came off me just like that. And I was hungry. Alright; I thought I knew one halal café, so I was going there. I came out and headed there, crossed the road, and then I suddenly saw my friends out of the corner of my eye. How they got wind of who they'd left to follow me in The Hamburg I'll never know, and I didn't have time to find out. I had to escape before they noticed me as they were just approaching the Mercure. Well, I dashed around the corner and ran. By then it was evening already. What kind of halal café would I be able to go to? I would be spotted in a second, just like in any halal store. That meant I had only what, fruits and veggies? But all the produce stores were closed and there were only minimarts, but I still needed to find them. So, I found one around ten, and I bought bananas and oranges.'

'Why not apples, tomatoes, and cucumbers? They are somewhat cheaper and more nutritious.'

'And where am I going to wash those cucumbers and apples? All the public toilets were closed already. Anyway, I grabbed that food and went to a lawn near Liedeshalle, the concert hall not far from you.'

'Thanks for the clarification. That concert hall is well known, even to those who live far from it.'

'Near that hall there's an underground walkway… or tunnel. There are all sorts of machines… for games and drinks. I got into that walkway and tried to sleep there. But how? You can't sleep on the concrete floor, but up there on the grass – sleep as much as you want. But it was too scary: what if my dear friends turned up there? But I didn't get through the night — I went out onto that grass and collapsed at once. For three hours,

I suffered from nightmares and jumped up with the first rays of the sun. Marion, darling, can I live at your place? I can't stay outside.'

'Well, I'm not against it,' the girl smirked; 'but what would my husband say?'

…The clip-clopping of her heels was fading and fading, and Hamid, who was rooted to the spot, still could not move, and only when Marion's figure dived under the marquee of the front entrance of The Hamburg did it even occur to him that she could at least bring him his things from the room. It was unlikely that this would require the permission of her husband – be he mythical or real. On the other hand, well, she could bring out his things for him, but where would he keep them? Where would he go at all?

***

Ta-TA-ta ta-TA-ta ta-TA-ta ta-TA-ta
Ta-TA-ta ta-TA-ta ta-TA-ta ta-TA
Ta-TA-ta ta-TA-ta ta-TA-ta ta-TA-ta
Ta-TA-ta ta-TA-ta ta-TA-ta ta-TA

"La Campanella," here?" he almost cried hearing the tune he adored in Schloßplatz – the central square of Stuttgart where the public wandered, where everything in the world was briskly sold, from cola and chewing gum to expensive souvenirs and albums with reproductions of Munch. On the other hand, why shouldn't the sounds of the divine violin of the great Niccolo resound in beautiful Germany, the bright Castal land from where the blessed rains of music and philosophy had fallen on the world more than once?

Listening to Paganini, Hamid completely forgot about Hamas, Fatah, IDF, ISIS… It seemed that one planet could not hold them all and "La Campanella." It seemed that the sound of "La Campanella" was one hundred percent proof that evil on the Earth was impossible and there was only music and love.

He walked closer to a group of people standing in a semicircle listening to the violin and found that they weren't only listening, but also watching. The real violinist remained in the background, and a young guy in a cap in front pulled the strings of a puppet figurine of a violinist in a tuxedo who moved the bow absolutely in time with the music. The boy handled the puppet with such virtuosity that not only did he create the impression he was playing himself, but it also seemed that somehow the puppet's facial expressions were changing. And yet … it would still be better if these two, and counting the doll, three, would choose something else, and not his beloved "La Campanella" as the subject of this parody.

Hamid decided not to finish listening to the desecrated "La Campanella" till the end and moved on across the huge square. All of a sudden, he didn't care what would happen to him. Let them catch him, and, well, kill him. At least something would happen — otherwise, there was just emptiness. Homeless, as they call it in English, and completely redundant. All he needed to do was to rot in the pedestrian tunnel or on the grass near the Liedeshalle.

'Endschuldigen mir bitte, sind Sie ein Araber?'

'Wh-what?'

'Excuse me, are you an Arab?'

An elderly albino woman (or maybe she was a blondie blond) was speaking to him with a thick accent, but still fairly well. He would have guessed that she was maybe seventy-five. She knocked on his shoulder as if knocking on a door.

'Arab,' Hamid muttered.

'Are you by any chance from Palestine?' the old woman glanced at him hopefully.

'From Palestine,' Hamid nodded.

'Maybe even from Gaza?'

Not believing her luck, the albino sighed.

'From Gaza,' Hamid agreed.

'There!' the old lady exclaimed triumphantly, addressing dozens of people gathered around a Palestinian flag and a placard that read: "Hands off Gaza," all of which Hamid hadn't noticed, so submerged was he in his thoughts.

'There!' she repeated. 'This person before us is directly from Gaza.'

The small crowd clapped with respect. Apparently, Hamid complied with the ideal image of the victim of Israeli aggression with his exhausted appearance and his dirty shirt.

'What's your name?' the blondie asked in a low voice.

'Hamid Shafi. Only I wouldn't like to…'

'Dear Hamid Shafi!' the old lady exclaimed, taking a few steps back and standing on some sort of platform, the pedestal of a greenish monument of medium size which Hamid had only noticed just now. 'Dear Hamid, before we ask you to tell us about the heroic struggle of your people, let us express on behalf of all the progressive powers of Germany, our support for this fight and wrath and indignation at the barbarities of Israeli.'

Truly they say: 'the rattling of a drum is heard from afar.'

Hamid looked at the faces of the "progressive powers." Undeniably, half of them were of Muslim origin, though it was unlikely they were Palestinian judging by the delight the old lady had expressed when she learned about his origin. The other half were clearly German, and not ordinary Germans; they were all well-matched, not only tow-headed but almost copies of that old woman, blondes, almost albinos.

As the old woman backed away towards the monument to the unknown German, Hamid began to move in the opposite direction, looking to escape. It was all in vain, though. Two of the old woman's companions – one blond and the other an Arab - began to push him from both sides towards the pedestal platform.

'Well, Hamid,' the old woman smiled encouragingly, 'tell us about your struggle, about your courage, about your hopes, and ... well, about your enemies.'

Suddenly, Hamid felt a surge of anger — and what anger!

'Oh, they are such bitches! You say enemies?' he shouted, literally hopping onto the platform. 'Alright, I'm going to tell you about enemies. I mean, we have an enemy. The main enemy. It's horrendous. And it has a name...' Hamid paused, as if wanting his audience to guess; "its name is Hamas!'

Though there was silence a minute ago and now there was silence too, they were two different types of silence. A second ago, four dozen eyes were looking at their guest from Gaza with interest, their lips smiling approvingly. And now there were four dozen frowning eyebrows with clenched fists, gritted jaws, and the silence of the brooding thundercloud. Well, silence it was, and Hamid fell silent too. A minute or more passed in that silence.

'We don't like Hamas that much either,' the old woman hissed, 'but we're for the Palestinian people!'

'I am the Palestinian people!' Hamid shouted. 'Are there any Palestinians here?'

He looked around the audience. Silence again. But it was a third type of silence — the silence of the tuck-tails.

'We support your wants and needs, your aspirations,' the old blond woman stated hesitatingly. 'We know that the Palestinian people want to have their own state…'

'But, I mean, the Palestinian people don't need any state! Palestinian people want one thing only — to live peacefully and quietly, and to earn money and raise their children. And most of all, the Palestinian people want the European legislators who came to terms with the Hamas terrorists to die as soon as possible!'

***

Compared to Palestine, Stuttgart was the far north, and in the north, as is well known, in summer it gets dark late. When the enraged Hamid got off the tram, the sun was still shining brightly, though it was already lodging in the west. In the slightly sloping rays, the concert hall looked like a huge horseshoe that had fallen to the ground adjacent to Berliner Platz.

"So, here I am at home," thought Hamid, dragging his feet wearily across the short-cut lawn, which at night in the rays of the moon he had mistaken for a glade.

He was at home. He would sit on the prickly grass and eat raw fruit and vegetables until his dear friends, to whom if it hadn't reached them yet, the explosive news of his performance would, of course, come very soon, would find him and complete what the Arabs and Jews had failed to complete there, on the shores of the Mediterranean Sea.

Pigeons were idling around the lawn; a lot of pigeons. If he concentrated on their Brownian motion, his head might have started spinning. And suddenly, the Brownian motion stopped. Chirping something inexplicable, or rather, simply squealing and gurgling, as Hamid thought with anger, they moved in his direction, though not only in his direction, but directly at him. Hamid stepped back before realising that they were demanding he feed them. There was only one way of feeding them — to go to the nearest store, buy more buns, and crumble them up for the birds. It took him about half an hour, but it still wasn't easy to feed them. The birds were hopping on him, trying to peck the bread out of his hands. When the birds calmed down, though, perhaps realising there was enough for everyone, he started enjoying seeing them busily pecking at the bread that he'd bought them.

Lying down on the grass, Hamid thought he would have to include this in his regular budget — feeding the blue-grey hosts of that ground.

"It's like paying rent," he smirked.

***

Hamid awoke to a hard blow on his side. A kick, to be exact, with a sharp boot tip. He opened his eyes. Two men were standing above him.

'Well, well, son of a swine, get up if you're a real man.'

"Now he's going to say: 'Get up to get what you deserve,' Hamid thought. "Is this nightmare going to haunt me every night now?"

Right, it was a nightmare, though alas, not a dream at all. Those two were real, their boots were real, and their fists were also real. There was only one consolation — they were beating him with half the strength, a somewhat prophylactic beating. And they were saying: 'There, son of a bitch. That's what you get, asshole. Next time, it will be even worse!'

"I mean, it would be good if there is no next time," Hamid thought. "But I have the Instruction. I need to give it to the world if they don't find it."

'You shouldn't have run from us,' the bigger guy pronounced when the beating was over.

Hamid recognised him as one of the four who came after him with Gamal. He was sitting on the lawn covered in dew. His head was humming, and blood was streaking from his burst lip. The "baboon face" squatted next to him.

'Does it hurt?' he asked almost compassionately.

Hamid attempted to nod, but the acute pain in his nape didn't allow him to.

'It does,' he said, barely moving his lips.

'Next time, it will be even more painful,' the "baboon face" continued. 'We might even kill you.'

'Why wait then?' the other guy, who looked quite miserable with his foxy face, chimed in. 'Let's finish him now, right here, and not even clear up afterwards. They'll find him and write it off for PEGIDA. It's trendy to accuse these sons of whores of all the sins.'

Hamid glanced at him. This despicable guy was speaking quite seriously, like an engineer suggesting an efficiency proposal in front of a board of directors.

'Well, why kill him at once?' the "baboon face" rebuked his colleague. 'We aren't animals, are we?'

"You are, indeed," Hamid thought.

'We'll have time to kill him later,' the "baboon face" continued. 'As they say, "death is a goblet that no one can avoid drinking from." First, we need to talk to the person… find out what air he breathes in. And if he breathes incorrectly, we need to convince him to breathe correctly. Allah commanded all of his creations to be merciful, and he isn't simply a creation, he's a true believer.'

'So, dear,' he then addressed Hamid, 'pack your duds if you have any and get lost from Stuttgart.'

'Where to?' Hamid whispered.

'Over the hills and far away,' he laughed, 'while you're still alive. Let's go, Mahmud!' he shouted to his companion. And when they were already in the distance, he slurred back over his shoulder to Hamid: 'You have two hours. Then we'll check.'

***

'And Paracelsus lived in this house.'

'Who is Paracelsus?' Hamid asked. That is, he would have asked if he hadn't learnt he needed to ask as few questions as possible. He'd been living in that weird city for two days, if it could be called living, the city, which was as if it had leapt from the pages of *One Thousand and One Nights* and cosily landed between the concrete masses of the Mercedes concern that surrounded it from all the sides. During those two days, Hamid had managed to grasp that the snobbery of local Arabs, at least those he'd communicated with, was simply too much. The one who had probably just found out about Martin Luther or even that same Paracelsus only yesterday, today was amazed: "How? Don't you know who Paracelsus is?"

'And Paracelsus lived in this house,' Munthir repeated, Hamid's new acquaintance, a guy of about thirty, tall and lean like a minute hand of a clock.

Hamid raised his eyes. The house was indeed remarkable. It was neat, white with perpendicular brown framings and rectangular windows. Pictures adorned the façade — there was some exotic bird with eighteen wings on the top floor, and below it there was a portrait of a man in a blue caftan and a medieval cap. For some reason, Hamid decided that this was how the mysterious Paracelsus must have looked like. The bird was on the white background and Paracelsus on a golden one. Those were either fresco paintings or tessera; he could not discern from below.

***

Did Hamid think that jumping at random into a commuter train that was rushing away from Stuttgart without the slightest idea where he was going and where he would get off, that in a small, as if painted Esslingen he would find, if not mental, then at least physical, peace? A casual conversation in the car and he was already on an unfamiliar platform, and then in the company of people who were also unfamiliar but looking at him with obvious sympathy. Anwar and his wife were from Hebron, and Munthir was a Syrian. They had lived in Esslingen for a long time and they were not very interested in politics, but when the Stuttgart Muslims had marched in solidarity with struggling Gaza through the streets of their city calling for the destruction of Israel two weeks ago, all three took an active part in this action and in pickets throughout the city. Now, Munthir gave Hamid a little tour.

'The cobblestone road here is beautiful,' Hamid said wistfully as they approached a little bridge over a river on the banks of which willows were dangling, and between them, flowers were sparkling in different colours.

'Yeah, the cobblestone pavement is wonderful here, Subhan Allah,' his companion exclaimed with such pride as if it was him who had lain that road himself. 'They laid it relatively recently, only a few decades ago, but they preserved the exact old pattern — see? It goes in certain waves. And on the Town Hall Square, we're going there now, there/s an ancient roadway that is three or four hundred years old, maybe even more.'

They came to a small bridge. Grey ducks were slowly moving towards each other on the quiet surface of the river. It seemed as if they were enjoying the coolness, so unusual for August, which was nonetheless reigning there despite the complete calmness in the air.

'Water…' Hamid sighed. 'Where is justice? Why do we suffer from thirst in Palestine, and here there are rivers, coolness, plants so juicy and so exuberant, not like the ones we have?'

'Allah is fair, it's true,; Munthir rebuked him. 'And if we live in harder conditions than people of other faiths, then it is His divine plan.'

"Divine plan?" Hamid thought. "Then why did you move to the north, breaking that plan, to these lands of those people of other faiths?"

Out loud, though, he said in a tone of reconciliation: 'Alright, let's go, you'll show me the Town Hall Square. You promised.'

The Town Hall Square was truly beautiful. The Gothic buildings looked like Egyptian pyramids, only with chopped-off sides and of different colours, from red, crimson, and pink to yellow and chartreuse. They seemed to be some stage settings for a performance from an ancient and quiet life.

'What is that?' Hamid asked, pointing at exquisite golden arrows that spread like rays on that pavement from a circle of the same colour in the centre of which something was written in German.

'Look attentively,' Munthir advised.

Hamid looked closer. There were names of cities above each arrow — Warsaw, Brest, Paris… Next to them, there were three-digit numbers, apparently the distance from Esslingen to those cities.

'This is cool,' Hamid said delightedly.

'Yep,' Munthir agreed, 'and in forty-fourth, right on this spot, there stood local Jews who were gathered here by the order of Esslingen authorities and were wondering where they'd be sent. Maybe here,' Munthir said, pointing at an arrow with the tip of his boot, above which was written, "Praha." 'Or maybe here?' he poked at an arrow indicating Vienna with his foot. 'And what if here?' the Arab said, turning one hundred and eighty degrees and directing the dreams of the Esslingen Jews towards Paris. 'But, alas, our dear relatives went via Yakub and Ishmael not here, and not here, and not here, but over there,' and he pointed at the cloudless blue sky with his finger. 'Thanks to which the number of potential invaders of our land diminished by several thousand.'

'Don't you pity them?' Hamid asked him, at a loss.

'And do you pity the ancestors of those who killed your children?' Munthir replied in the same tone.

"Hamas killed my children," Hamid thought, though he didn't say anything.

Moshe's face appeared before him, and for some reason he imagined the tanned Jew standing on that same spot wrapped in a raincoat, and the sky above him was not blue but grey with rain pouring heavily, and Moshe was embracing his wife who was originally from Russia, and they were cuddling together as they were both cold, cold, cold, and the sky was throwing not drops of water anymore, but millions of needles, icy and at the same time burning hot, and those needles were sticking in them and biting Moshe and his wife and other people who were like Moshe and his wife, standing under that horrid rain, that hail of icy needles, and those people were shouting and crying, and there were hundreds and thousands of men and women, men and women; and each man had Moshe's tanned face, and each woman had Moshe's wife's face. Then Hamid clearly smelt tobacco smoke. "Who's smoking?" Ah, that man in a beautiful SS uniform with a clean-cut face and shaved temples.

"Where are you taking us?" Moshe asked, and all the Moshe's asked in unison, and his wife, their wives responded: "War will tell the further plan."

***

'And this house here, do you see, the villa with a rooster on the roof… nice, right? And the turret is joyful. This house was actually built recently, but it looks ancient. So, this is where our friend…'

'Whose "ours?"' Hamid interrupted his guide.

'"Ours" means of our people. Here lives a friend of our people, the famous journalist Herman Schroder. Though he is not an Arab, he…'

'Wh-what?' Hamid lost his breath. 'Herman Schroder? "Ulenspiegel?"'

'See?' Munthir replied carelessly. 'I'm telling you — he's famous. Even you've heard of him? I'm not personally acquainted with him, but Yassir, the head of our group, knows him very well. With time, I'll introduce you to Yassir, and Yassir will introduce you to Ulenspiegel. You're going to have interesting topics to discuss.'

"With time?" Hamid thought with indignation. "Should I wait until then, right? Eh, Hamid, have you forgotten a pearl of old Arabic wisdom: 'If you managed to escape a lion, then stop hunting for it.' And on the other hand, there is another proverb: 'A drenched person is not afraid of rain.'"

**

'Shower, changing clothes, all later,' said Ulenspiegel. 'Now you, as you look exhausted after your journey, are going to sit on that stool over there… No, no, not the armchair, but particularly the stool. You should understand that right now you are not a man; what I mean to say is not a simple man: you are an icon. The icon of the Palestinian's people's sufferings! Yes, yes, sit over there; excellent! I'll turn on the camera, and you start your story.'

Hamid looked around. It would be much nicer to be sitting in the armchair. The armchair was antique, with armrests decorated with carvings. The same carvings adorned the bookcases. If someone sat in such an armchair, he would associate himself with the horde of those who wrote those volumes plunging into the calm centuries…

'Well,' Herman asked impatiently.

Hamid had dreamt about this encounter so much, but now he was at a loss. This was not how he'd imagined the Ulenspiegel. Where was that hawk-like facial profile? Where were the eyes filled with pain for the miserable citizens of Shudjaia? There was a bald man with shaven temples fidgeting in front of him. It looked like this man was trying to arrange some sort of performance. And indeed, why did it matter where Hamid sat? Would his pain for Aya, Mamduh, Muhammad, and Ahdaf lessen if he sat in the armchair? Would the tragedy stop being a tragedy if he took a shower? But the main thing wasn't in that — if a man came to you with his grief, you should sit and talk to him if you were the real Ulenspiegel, if the blood of innocent victims really pounded in your heart. Why are you grasping at your camera all at once? And that joyous squeal: 'Are you from Shudjaia directly?' It sounded as if he'd asked: 'Are you straight from the White House?' "I'm not an icon at all," Hamid thought, completely worn out. "Icon's children don't perish." Some weird feeling of wariness of an unknown origin didn't allow him to take out the holy Instruction from under his shirt. "Later," he whispered to himself in his mind. "Later. I need to get used to him. We'll talk and then…"

Herman listened to Hamid's story very attentively, though, obviously, due to his nature, he couldn't sit still for a second. He either jumped up and then sat back down, adjusted the camera, or checked the level of sound in the microphone. Only when Hamid told him that right before the attack the Jews warned him and his neighbours on the phone, and for those, whose phone numbers they didn't know they specially spread leaflets, the journalist stopped the camera and said cringing: 'This fairy tale is often told. We shouldn't repeat it once again.'

'I mean, it's not a fairy tale…' Hamid started indignantly.

'Maybe, maybe…' Ulenspiegel interrupted him. 'Then it's just a propaganda trick. They know you have nowhere to go.'

'They do,' Hamid agreed. 'I mean, but what can they do?'

'Not shoot,' the German said simply.

Hamid couldn't find the words to answer that. But the journalist, unravelling his attack, continued: 'I don't mean to idealise Hamas, but this is still the people's war. Even children rose to the occasion to fight.'

'Yeah,' Hamid answered. 'They rose. At the behest of Hamas, they run up to soldiers asking for help, saying that someone is feeling bad somewhere, or that someone twisted his ankle, or something else, and those kind-hearted guys go to the tunnel at their request and get blown up there. This is correct, you know, I'm saying it as a teacher.'

'Kind-hearted Jews? But they're murderers!'

Hamid suddenly felt such an unearthly weariness. He instantly wanted to be somewhere far from there, it didn't matter where, though most of all at the sea, his very own the Mediterranean Sea, and particularly ON the sea, not near it, but on the blue-green-golden smooth surface that only seemed to be ripple, but it held one much tighter than the elusive European lands. Probably, he shouldn't hurry with the story about the Instruction…

The European guy felt he'd been somewhat too pushy with his anti-Jewish insults. That Arab, with his strange affinities towards the Israeli people, didn't remind him of any others he'd met before. He said in a reconciliatory manner: 'I'm not going to condone those Hamas guys. Any way you slice it, at the end of the day, they're still terrorists.'

'Terrorists?' Hamid exclaimed, exasperated by the way Ulenspiegel squeezed that confession with some reservation out of himself. 'I mean, they're butchers! If only you knew how many they executed. Even among my friends — Ali Suyef, Muhammad Husseini, and Firaz Traira! They were executed just because they had Israeli mobile phones with them. And Hashem and Nur, and other five guys were shot when they came out to the street with the demand "Silence in return of silence." And do you know that our people disappear forever based on a neighbour's delation, saying that the person was heard to have anti-Hamas conversations? And that we have big two new prisons that were recently built and they're both overcrowded now? And that Hamas guys rape women and then throw them into prisons for adultery, and that they beat uncovered girls with sticks right in the middle of the street, that they drive around the city on motorbikes, Land Rovers and Mercedes that they stole in Israel with bludgeons in their hands, attacking anyone they see just for fun?'

'Alright, let's leave them alone. Now, tell me how your children perished.'

And again — how calmly he pronounced that.

But he couldn't do anything about it; the journalist had already switched on his camera, and Hamid unwillingly started narrating. However, he was becoming more inspired bit by bit.

Ulenspiegel listened attentively to how the Hamas soldiers dragged the children to the roof of an apartment house, how they brought a missile launcher, how he tried to save his children, how he was thrown out and manhandled, and how the retaliatory Israeli missile turned everyone who was on the roof into a dark red mush right in front of his eyes. How he found one hand of little Maruan, how foreign television guys arrived then, how he'd tried to explain to them what had happened in reality, how the TV guys decided not to listen to him, how the Hamas guys were beating him, and how during the funeral he was trying to tell what had really happened once again in vain. How five days later he was arrested by Hamas's people. He spoke about how a man in a balaclava was interrogating him with such commitment, and how he saved himself thanks to the savings he got during those five days by turning out the pockets of the deceased and looting abandoned or bombed-out apartments.

'I mean, when I was doing that,' Hamid clarified, 'I knew I would meet you or someone who'd help me tell the world about what Hamas is doing one day. That was my duty in regard to those whose corpses and apartments I was reefing. But it turned out that this money was used to free myself. On getting out of there without a penny, I was in despair. You might ask why — like, I could have started turning out pockets and looting apartments again. Alas, during the time I spent in confinement, there were so many people who'd lost everything and were living by marauding in the streets, and all the pockets and apartments, both those unbroken and destroyed, were all empty. Oh, how I prayed to Allah so that He would help me achieve something for the sake of which I should stay alive. Every night I prayed, going to bed among concrete blocks with pieces of rusty reinforcement sticking out of them, every day wandering among the same blocks in search of a coin lying around somewhere or at least something to eat. And then one day, on the way to the mosque, amongst the wreckage of a kiosk where sweets and Coca-Cola were once sold, I saw a piece of a newspaper in English. The headline read: "Stuttgart journalist Ulenspiegel: The ashes of Shudjaia pound in my heart."'

'I remember that article,' Ulenspiegel muttered.

'I mean, I read it and cried,' Hamid continued. 'I cried because the words you wrote were burning my heart, I cried because when I read it I saw the faces of Aya and my babies, I cried because I realised there was someone out there who cared about the destinies of the miserable people of Shudjaia, I cried because I understood that unfortunately, without a penny in my pocket, I wouldn't be able to meet you and tell you the whole truth. And then… then I went to Abu Ain Mosque for a maghrib, an evening prayer, and when everyone started leaving, I got up on the minbar, it's a raised platform from which an imam reads khutbakh…'

'Khutbakh?'

'Well, the sermon. So, I hid behind the minbar so that Mullah didn't see me… I mean, all night, do you hear me, all night I prayed to Allah to help me get to Stuttgart. And in the morning, when salat al-fajr was over…'

'Can you please explain what "salat al-fajr" is?' Ulenspiegel interrupted.

'"Salat al-fajr" is our morning prayer between the dawn and the sunrise. So, when the salat al-fajr was over, I left the Mosque and the first person I ran into was Sari al-Farane, with whom I spent time in prison. Sari was a stalwart fighter against Hamas, a desperate Fatah member and a friend of Abu-Mazen.'

'Well yeah, and those pictures were so horrible…'

'I mean, the Israeli seamen had nothing to do with it. I don't know who killed the other three, but Azzam, Sari's son, was shot by Hamas's people while Sari was in jail. Those bastards are such good psychologists. They took him as if for interrogation and said he had seven sons and here is the first one. If you continue doing such things, the other six will follow him. That was his favourite son… but it didn't matter. I remember al-Farane in prison. He was tall and proud… one day when I was walking near the interrogation room, and I mean, you wouldn't believe it, I myself it heard - Allah won't allow me to lie - I heard his laughter from behind the door. The other prisoners said, and I don't know whether it's true or not, that he was laughing in the Hamas' people's faces even as he was being beaten by them. And then… when I met him after the jail… he was walking all hunched up and depressed. And when he spoke, he was shaking. Well, not all — when he spoke about Azzam his lips were trembling, and when he spoke of the other kids who were still alive, his fingers were shaking. And all the time he was looking around, looking around… "That's it," he said; "Hamid, I'm done." I mean, I told him about you and said I was going to see you and tell you the truth, but I had no money to get to you. He looked at me so suspiciously and said: "You were picking shekels from pockets and roaming through empty houses."

"'Yeah," I said, "and all those shekels landed in Hamas guys' pockets, otherwise, how do you think I got free, huh?" He looked at me from under his brow and said: "I have money; less than before, but still enough. I wish there was no money and Azzam was here instead. There's enough for you and your passport, clothes, ticket, hotel, and food; just get to that Ulenspiegel of yours and tell him everything. Do you hear me? Tell him everything!" I said: "Thank you." And he started shouting: "What the hell do you mean 'thank you?' You're doing this for me! Do you understand? For me!" And also, Sari gave me…'

'How did you get out of Gaza?' Herman interrupted to ask in a dry voice.

'I mean, via a tunnel,' Hamid replied. 'Via the Hamas tunnel, where I came across the corpse of a twelve-year-old boy just three hundred meters from the entrance. Probably one of those who was digging it — he either died during the construction or was put out of commission as a witness.'

'And what happened to you when you got to Israel?' There was some liveliness in the journalist's voice, and maybe even a secret hope that now there would be something about the cruelty of the Zionists.

'I mean, Moshe, a Jew from Iraq, he sheltered me. I rested at his place, slept a little, and went to the airport. Hamas's people chased me in Stuttgart, but I found you anyway, Ulenspiegel. Our blood and our pain pound in your heart. Inform the whole world that the cause of all our calamities is HAMAS! And there is something else…'

He wanted to speak about the Instruction that had gotten into Sari's hands - nobody knew how - and that Sari had given to him to share with the world, and about the other instruction, which was not so secret but also valuable, that he saved from his brother in faith in the café where they ate shawarma. He wanted… but then he met the eyes of Herman Schroder and turned pale. The eyes of the latter were tinted with such wild and undisguised malice.

'What else?' Schroder said from between his gritted teeth.

'E-r-r… nothing.'

***

'Coffee without cardamom is not coffee,' Rasmi uttered thoughtfully.

Hamid was about to voice his agreement, but his mouth was occupied with TAMIYA, balls rolled from bean-garlic puree mixed with finely chopped boiled eggs and fried in vegetable oil. Based on how masterfully Rasmi cooked that dish, which was not so popular among the inhabitants of Gaza that came to the eastern Mediterranean region from neighbouring

Egypt, he was also originally from Cairo, like Gamal.

'Rasmi, where are you from?' he asked.

'I was born in Fureidis.'

'In Fureidis?' Hamid asked, bewildered. That was the last thing he'd he expected - Rasmi, an assistant of Herman Schroder, was originally from a town just a few dozens of kilometres from Gaza in the middle of Israel. It was well known that there are practically no Arabs of Israeli citizenship migrating to Europe. Why would they need Europe? In general, Rasmi was a weird guy — he had the manners of a refined European person, but he worked at Herman Schroder's as the help. Now it turned out that he'd immigrated here from Israel.

'Rasmi, why did you leave Fureidis?'

'I didn't get along with the neighbouring hamula,' Rasmi said curtly, and the topic was closed. The question of where Rasmi had got the knack of cooking Egyptian cuisine, Hamid decided not to raise.

"Where did Schroder go so unexpectedly? He took out a sim-card from the camera and left," he thought.

'Let's go, I'll show you your room,' he heard Rasmi saying.

It was unlikely that this staircase was so long in truth, but it seemed endless for Hamid. He decided not to ask Rasmi why the room that Schroder had given him was in the basement. "Well, then the basement it is… but why is it so sombre? Concrete walls with pipes sticking out from them, and some metal sticks as grey as the walls." Suddenly, Hamid was overwhelmed by the feeling he was going to die, and that death seemed to him not like some black abyss, as one usually imagined it, but like dusk, grey as that concrete.

The room he entered wasn't a room at all. It was simply a part of the basement, only the walls there were not concrete but made of brick. They were mixed with thick layers of cement, lumpish bits of which were hanging like petrified grey clouds.

"And where is a table, a chair or a bed?" Hamid was about to ask when a rope flickered in front of his eyes, and he immediately felt as if someone's terrifying fingers were squeezing his throat. He jerked, but the garrotte stung into his neck even tighter. Everything became blurry, and he suddenly felt an inexplicable sense of bliss. It seemed to him that his hands were caressing a woman's body…

'Aya…' he whispered. But it was not Aya. Marion's black hair was covering him in waves. It entangled and filled everything around him, and it all became black… black… black… And then sudden pain, again; the pain that squeezed his throat. At the same time, in the darkness that was filling his eyes, he saw a patch of light. The grey lumps of the petrified cement and red bricks appeared from the dark. How long did it last? Eternity? A moment? Eventually, he found out that it was a moment. The moment that Rasmi need-ed to let the garrotte go from his hands and fall on the rough cement floor, drooling with bloody bubbles. For a few minutes, Hamid sat on the dark grey floor, coughing so hard that his eyes were welling up. He bluntly looked at Rasmi's nape covered in black with grey slightly curly hair, at his wide back in the brat check shirt, and at the big beautiful and curvy dag-ger with a pearled handle that was protruding from his back. Then the shirt became deep red in colour, and the brat check wasn't discernible in that pool of redness anymore. Hamid coughed so hard that he threw up on that dark cement floor. Or maybe he threw up not because of the cough, but because of the view of that murderer, Rasmi.

He was afraid to raise his eyes; afraid to look at whomever had saved his life. He only saw how a leg in jeans and an Adidas sneaker turned Rasmi's body on his back with a strong movement. Hamid heard the thud of the nape on the cement floor and the sound of the dagger's handle, that same pearled one, scratching that floor. He vomited again.

'A thousand dicks in your ass!' the voice sounded familiar to Hamid.

'Why the hell did you stab him?'

'You're a faggot's bro!' was the response. "Who knew that it was his servant? It was you who whispered: "It's him."'

'I whispered it, but I didn't order you to kill him at once. And if you didn't, we could have asked that what's-his-name, Rasem, right? We could have asked where that Schroder is. And now, who should we ask? This dumbass of ours?'

Realising that 'dumbass' was in reference to him, Hamid finally forced himself to raise his eyes. In front of him was the same couple that had manhandled him at the Concert Hall. It was difficult to tell which of them was the leader and which was the follower. On the one hand, the "baboon face" spoke like the obvious boss and scolded the despicable Mahmud like a naughty schoolboy, but on the other the despicable one was clearly closer to the authorities and more knowledgeable because in response to the slap down he calmly said: 'You don't understand a thing, Abbas. The problem is that happened too fast. Gamal calls me and says: "You need to take Schroder down. He became impudent, so much so that he decided to blackmail us. Go, guys, to Esslingen and deal with him there and with that son of a swine, the truth-seeker that came back again like a bad shilling…"

'Hey, friend,' he suddenly addressed Hamid. 'Do you have any idea where your benefactor is, that same Schroder?'

Hamid shook his head energetically. He felt nauseous because of the smell of his own puke. Suddenly, he started chuckling through tears at the thought of how delicious the Tamiya had looked on the plate and how unseemly it looked now in the form of a ginger-brown mess on the grey cement. And the aroma was significantly different then and now…

The "baboon face" interpreted his laughter in his own manner.

'You don't believe us,' he said scornfully. 'You think that if Gamal gave us orders to kill you, we're going to do it for sure? Try to understand, we're not murderers. Allah doesn't desire a sinner's death, but his repentance. You're driven by the idea that if we use the lives of Arab children as a weapon in the fight with the enemy that the blood of these children — your children, our children is on our hands, right?'

Unable to pronounce a word, Hamid just nodded.

'But it's not right, see?' the big-faced Abbas exclaimed with passion. 'Those who left us without any other weapon are to blame. Those who hold us under siege, leave us devoid of all rights and don't consider us as people. And such types as that Schroder, they're with us only until we pay them, and as soon as we turn our back on them, they'd be ready to stab us.'

"I mean, it was you who was going to stab him in the back," Hamid thought, "but stabbed his servant instead." Out loud, though, he said, or to be exact, squeezed out:

'Maybe… maybe, Ulenspiegel simply didn't understand what is going on in reality…'

'Oh, come on!' the one with a fox face interrupted. "As if Schroder didn't know about the human shields before!'

'And what do you think… our friend… err… Hamid,' Abbas cut in; "on whose order did that Rasem, Schroder's servant, try to kill you? You think it was mine, or on his own initiative? Maybe it was Mr Schroder himself, who, having got the recordings of the talk with you, decided to blackmail us and get rid of you so he wouldn't lose his exclusive? Huh? You're silent, now? See for yourself - we saved your life. If not for us, you'd be quietly cooling down here in this basement with a garrotte around your neck. And all we need now is you to tell us where Schroder is and give us your word as a "thank you" that you're not going to stand against us.'

'I mean it, I don't know where Ulens… where Schroder is,' Hamid wheezed. 'And not to stand against you…' he started coughing again, and that seemed to settle his destiny.

'Stop chatting with him!' the despicable one hissed. 'Orders are orders. As they say, an empty well won't be filled with dew. If there are no clouds, there won't be rain.'

'Satan knows! And what if he knows, as they say, where cassis grows…' Abbas uttered hesitatingly.

'He doesn't know a thing,' Mahmud squealed. 'Enough! We'll be stuck here for ages.'

'Alright…'

The "baboon face" grabbed Hamid by the hair, and with a jerk, raised him to his feet. Hamid tried to step back, but who could escape the grasp of the "baboon face?" With one hand, he pulled Hamid's arms behind his back, and with the other, he held him by the hair. Abbas pulled him so his head fell back, exposing his throat to the exquisitely curved knife with the pearled handle, which the one with the fox face, having turned Rasmi's body face down again, had pulled from the dead man's back.

Hamid closed his eyes. This was how it was going to end then. Since his childhood, he'd tried to imagine now and again how he would die one day, how he would transit into death. He'd tried to imagine what death was like, and lately he'd often thought about that strange land where Aya and Mamduh, Muhammad, and Ahdaf had moved onto. And now, standing on the threshold of that land, the main feeling he experienced was fatigue. A mortal, in all senses, fatigue, and also… also disappointment. Right there, right now, in that filthy basement, in the knowledge that the last moment of his life was about to pass, Hamid realised the worst… that Ulenspiegel, that Ulenspiegel in whom he had so desperately believed in, that same Ulenspiegel who he'd dreamt of meeting, that particular Ulenspiegel was the reason why his children had perished. For the sake of that Ulenspiegel, Hamas soldiers dragged those children onto the roof so they could be blown into pieces by the Israeli missile. As all those human shields wouldn't be worth two pence if it wasn't for that pack of journalists who would then describe the barbarity of the Jews, barbarities in which they didn't believe themselves, and shout about the ashes that allegedly pounded in their hearts, in their deceitful, cold, and pain-proof hearts. It was a pity that he'd realised this too late, a pity that he'd been led by a false light and walked into a swamp from where it was impossible to get out. And the Instructions? Maybe he should've given them to Schroder? With all his cynicism, he could have published them in pursuit of sensation.

A gunshot rung out very close, and then a second one. Still not realising what had happened, Hamid felt the hand that was holding his hair in a death grip help- lessly slip along his shoulder. He opened his eyes.

The "baboon face" lay on the concrete floor and twitched in his last convulsion. His arm with the club-fingers feebly scratched the floor, and a trickle of blood was oozing from the corner of his mouth. The owner of the fox face lay with a hole in his forehead and looked to the ceiling as if in surprise. It looked like he'd managed to turn back after all. Instantaneously, Hamid's head started hurting, especially at the roots of his hair, which had almost been plucked out.

'We're going to bury these three and take off from here,' Herman Schroder said, setting the safety catch on the revolver.

Hamid rejoiced. He was right, after all! He was not mistaken about Ulenspiegel, who had saved his life! Ulenspiegel was a friend, after all! Together they would show Hamas in its true colours!

'There,' putting his hand under his shirt, he sol- emnly pulled out the plastic bag with the carefully folded, ill-fated Instruction. 'This document exposes

HAMAS!'

Ulenspiegel unwrapped the package, skimmed over the paper, then negligently put it into the inner pocket of his jacket, and pointing at the dead Abbas said, 'Let's do it.'

Hamid grabbed the body by the legs, assuming that the German would take it by the arms.

'Nah,' he grumbled, taking the corpse under the arms and lumbering it onto Hamid's back, which he readily offered. Then he took a spade from the corner and barked, 'Let's go!'

That 'let's go' was said in English, but it sounded like a purely German phrase, something from American movies about the war. It was strange, he spoke English before with a German accent, but there was nothing barking in his speech. And now...

The path came out from the backyard and crossed the street, which was paved with cubes, and led to a hillside. There was just one house on the way there, and luckily its windows were not lit.

'Everything is going well so far,' Schroder mumbled.

Hamid wanted to ask what would have happened if there was someone in the house.

'The owners left for a week,' Schroder outpaced him with his response.

Hamid calmed down but, not for long. There was something weird about Schroder's behaviour. Why did Ulenspiegel not grab the second corpse, but with a bossy gesture, silently make Hamid, who was literally shaking from exhaustion after he'd dragged the weighty body of the "baboon face," run back to get shabby Mahmud? Of course, he was much lighter than his friend, but still, wasn't the pain of the Palestinian people pounding in Ulenspiegel's heart? And if it was, then why he was treating Hamid, the son of that Palestinian people, as if he were a slave? It didn't fit with the bright image…

With these unpleasant thoughts, Hamid dragged all three corpses of his would-be executioners and unloaded them below a precipice on top of which stood Schroder with his arms akimbo in the classic pose of a coloniser from a caricature in a radical magazine from the sixties. He wiped away his sweat and, like a child waiting for approval, asked timidly: 'So, how did you like the Instruction?'

Instead of an answer, with a clink on a stone, a spade fell at his feet.

'Dig,' Schroder shouted. In his hand, apparently, as a means of defence in case Hamid decided to use that shovel for another purpose, he had that same gun which he'd used to kill the two cut-throats.

Hamid shrugged his shoulders - alright, after all Ulenspiegel had saved his life - and started digging a ditch. The last time he'd been given this order was three weeks ago, when he was commanded by a lady-like, hermaphrodite-looking Hamas soldier who was in charge of removing the rubble that had appeared after Israeli attacks the streets where Hamid happened to turn when he was going to get some pita. The Hamas guy attempted to growl with his squeaky voice, waved his hands, and Hamid and a couple of teenagers and a few silent women who were mobilized for clearing were soon dragging the stone blocks.

'Schneller!' Schroder bawled out.

The soil was not concrete, of course, but as if compressed, the top layer was easily removed, but then something began to grind under the tip of a shovel, and pieces of soil were barely peeled off. In general, every metre... but what is a meter... every centimetre was taken with a fight. Increasingly, Hamid seemed to lean on the shovel, slowing down the rhythm of his movements and simply resting.

'Schneller!' Schroder yelled then, completely transformed into an SS-man from an American movie about the Second World War or the Holocaust. An inexplicable awe overwhelmed Hamid then. He felt as if he was a Jew in hands of a slaughterer, a Jew from those pre-Israeli times.

"Eh," Hamid thought like a bolt from the blue, "If only Moshe was here. He would have…"

So there, the ditch was ready and quite deep, and now it needed to be turned into a trench, enough for three bodies.

Either Hamid got his second wind or he was so deep in his thoughts or something else, but the minutes, ten to be exact, during which the trench for three appeared passed almost without notice. It was like a minute ago he was evaluating and calculating to what extent to dig, and then he was already wiping his forehead and looking at Schroder inquiringly.

'Dig more!' Schroder shouted.

At first, Hamid thought he hadn't heard properly. "Dig more? Why? We just push the bodies off into the trench, and that's it."

"Dig, donner wetter!"

And how much wrath was there in that peremptory bark — and was it wrath or hatred? Hamid put down the shovel and gazed up. Right at that moment the moon, as if at the snap of the fingers of some unknown director, climbed out from behind a cloud and gave an even clearer outline of Ulenspiegel's black silhouette — the silhouette of a Hollywood villain.

Where did that berserk fury come from at the

man who'd saved him, saved Hamid's life just an hour and a half ago?

At that moment, the moon became merciful and poured its opalescent rays on the clear-cut with shaven temples face of the man, and Hamid realised why it seemed so familiar to him. It was the face of the SS-man from the vision he'd had in the Town Hall Square. He wished he could look into the man's eyes and understand why he hated him so much. What had Hamid done to him? But the moon was shining and both of his eyes were black hollows, thoroughly hiding everything kept behind them. But the third eye... Hamid knew what was behind the third eye, but it didn't make it easier, because the eye was the muzzle of the revolver, which was aiming directly at him. And this was the person who Hamid had come to himself willingly, and given the precious Instruction!

'Dig, scum!'

Hamid timidly lowered his eyes and was about to raise his foot to press the spade's blade down when he froze in amazement. And it was such amazement that for a second, well, not for a second, but for a particle of a second, he forgot about the muzzle of death aiming at him. He saw... a cat at own feet. An ordinary cat. And how could he not pay attention to it as he'd been walking around Stuttgart and Esslingen for a week and not seen a single cat in the streets, besides those that were walked on a leash, like the one near The Hamburg? He, who, when he was seven-years-old, with his sister Hanin, futilely tried to take care of a kitten that had gotten under the wheels of a bicycle. He, who until the last day of the existence of their house in Shudjaia, not only brought out some food that affectionate Aya prepared for the cats from the neighbourhood, but also bought ProPlan for cats himself in a local pet store. The store where Rico and Coco, the two cockatoos which were famous throughout Gaza for being addicted to coffee, lived, and drank several cups a day in front of the delighted visitors, one of whom he was quite often himself. All of them had perished — Hanin and Aya, and the animals and birds.

The moon disappeared behind a cloud before Hamid could discern what colour that creature was which was rubbing itself against his legs so trustfully. But Schroder must have had better vision and saw the cat even without the moon, because the shot that made Hamid jump out of his skin and the bat hiding in the branches of a sycamore growing on a slope dash into the darkness of the night… that shot was surprisingly accurate. With a whimper, the cat rushed to the side and plopped down into the freshly dug trench. The supple moon quickly slid from behind the cloud to light its body, from which black blood was pouring. Its paw jerked several times before becoming quiet forever, and its tail that it was still trying to move… And he remembered: "God forbid for me to live to the day when I have no more tears for a stray dog. I wish Moshe was here."

And maybe he wasn't such a good shot that Ulens… well, what the hell with Ulenspiegel? He was Schroder, a fascist German swine. So, what was he — a sharpshooter or a fumbler who got the cat accidentally as he wasn't aiming at the cat at all, but… then who, who was he aiming at? And then — the simplest thought dawned on him — amazing; how had it not occur to him before? "Why would that Rasmi, Schroder's servant, suddenly try to kill him? Wasn't it on the orders of Schroder himself? Then it meant that by shooting Abbas and Mahmud, Schroder wasn't saving Hamid at all, he was saving himself from the planted would-be killers! Remember, Hamid: "You need to take Schroder down. He became impudent so much that he decided to blackmail us. Go, guys, to Esslingen and deal with him there and with that son of a swine, the truth-seeker that came back again like a bad shilling…"

Hamid raised his eyes again. Schroder wasn't in a hurry. He was aiming calmly, taking his time. Hamid had nowhere to go anyway — he was standing in front of the killer in full view. And the moon, that bastard moon, like a good projector was lighting the victim with all its might as if saying — shoot, Herr Schroder.

Hamid squeezed his eyes. During the last three hours, he was going to be killed three times. Now there would be a shot.

But there was no shot. Instead, there was a weird sound — as if something big and heavy fell from a moderate height. Without waiting for the next shot, Hamid carefully opened his eyes and saw what had fallen from the slope. It was Schroder's body.

***

One of our wise books says: 'A sage who found a skull in the river said: "For the fact that you drowned someone, you were drowned, but the one drowning you will drown too." It was almost the same situation here. That Rasmi wanted to kill you, and those two killed him. Schroder shot them…'

'And you broke Schroder's neck with the edge of your hand,' Hamid finished, crossing his arms on his chest and embracing his shoulders. He still had the chills. 'Where did you learn that, huh?'

They were sitting on the same slope where half an hour ago Schroder stood with the face of an SS-man with the revolver in his hand.

'In "Sayeret Matkal,' Moshe replied. 'It wasn't that difficult. Approaching him stealthily from behind so he didn't hear was…'

'I mean, you're my saviour…' Hamid started.

'I explained to you already, I explained,' Moshe rebuked, 'that you are my saviour. If you hadn't run away that night and I hadn't chased you, hadn't chased you to the airport, I would have stayed home where a missile struck soon after, and I would've lain now, lain like these here…' he nodded in the direction of the just filled trench on top of which the soil protruded. 'I would've quietly lain somewhere. There wouldn't be a tombstone yet above me, and the grave would have been like an unsown lawn, and my grandchildren would have lined it with colourful pebbles.'

'Let it be so then,' Hamid agreed, chuckling. 'But all my previous saviours first saved me and then tried to kill me but did not succeed… I hope you're not going to follow in their steps.'

'What do you mean?'

'I mean, you're not going to try to kill me.'

'Oh, I thought you meant you hoped I would follow in their footsteps… meaning I wouldn't go to kingdom come right after my victim,' Moshe laughed.

'What are you talking about?' Hamid exclaimed almost seriously. 'How can that be? You — to kingdom come!'

'Why? Why not?' Moshe wondered. 'Am I God?'

'I mean, you are a demi-god,' Hamid uttered without a smile.

'Alright, demi it is,' Moshe agreed. 'By the way, where does it smell like cigarettes? There's no one here except us, I think.'

'I don't know,' Hamid responded. 'But it's a good idea. I probably have one.'

And reaching for a pack from his pocket, he took out a cigarette with a shaky hand.

'Well, have a smoke then,' Moshe approved while rising, and then suddenly he faltered. Right, it was that same smell which had haunted him and on the shore under Ashkelon, and at the airport, and in Pardes Hanna, and now it was here. It wasn't a simple odour of tobacco smoke; it was the scent of deliverance. They say that there is an odour of Death. Well, the tobacco smoke that Hamid exhaled bore the aroma of life. Moshe gently looked at that skinny guy who was sitting all hunched up, who was squatting and sucking on a cigarette, puff after puff. Well, don't melt now!

'How did you find me?' Hamid asked in a somewhat pitiful voice, glancing at the standing above him Moshe.

'I'll tell you later, there's no time now. It's time, time to go,' Moshe announced, stretching.

'Where to now? I mean, you were talking about Munich, right?' Hamid asked.

There was some humbleness, if not "predestination" in his voice. His previous saviours had set out to kill him before he even knew it. At least this one hadn't started with an attempt on his life, but now he was taking about taking him to hell, to Munich. What was he going to do in that damn Munich? It's not a coincidence that there's a pearl of folk wisdom that says: "If you follow an owl, you'll end up in ruins."

'We're going to Munich to meet the real Ulenspiegel, the person for whom a stranger's pain truly pounds in his heart. Unlike your Schroder,' he pointed in the direction of the trench, 'and other such Schroders that are the real killers of children in Gaza, that is, they're the commissioners of their death.'

'Leave Schroder alone,' Hamid said. 'As my people say, we do not reproach the dead.'

'That's right,' Moshe agreed, 'and he's not going to reproach us for anything after his death. Besides, at the end of the day, he has nothing to reproach us for. And as for Peter, he is a real honest journalist. He has an internet channel. Not central television, of course, but at least something. Let's go to the Audi.'

'What Audi?' Hamid asked.

'The Audi A6 that I rented first thing on my arrival in Stuttgart. I left it two blocks away from the house of your Schroder. Get up, there's no time to lose, no time.'

"Well," Hamid thought, "no time it is then. Let's go and look at that Peter. I mean, what if something comes out of it? As they say, roses come from thorns."

***

'That journalist is a Jew, of course?' Hamid asked.

'He's a German Christian, a member of an organisation that supports Israel. Wanna know how we met?'

'How?' Hamid asked in a tired voice. He was bewildered. He should be happy. Not just had he miraculously been saved by Allah three times within three hours, but now, when it seemed his hope to make his dream come true and tell the world the truth about what was really going on in Gaza and produce the Instruction he'd taken from Schroder's pocket before burying him - Allah was reviving that dream of his now - but he had no strength to enjoy it.

'Nine years ago, our Prime Minister, Ariel Sharon, destroyed the settlement zone around Gaza — Gush Katif. Do you remember?'

'How could I not remember that? We were so happy. "The Jews are running away!" "Intifada wins!" "Long live Hamas!" Only those who worked in the Israeli settlements and greenhouses cried.'

'I seeeee,' Moshe drawled, turning to the highway. 'And what about your sobering enlightenment?'

'I mean, it took us years. I once voted for Hamas myself. Besides, in the beginning we actually felt the alleviation — there were no more roadblocks. We could go anywhere we wanted. We felt like prisoners before — document checks with every step, and there were long queues that lasted for hours, the soldiers' abusive language… but how is your Christian friend… eeerrr….related to that?'

'Peter? I'll tell you. So, you were happy, and we, respectively, were terrified. We — were all those who reckoned that Jews had the right to live on their land…'

'On yours or someone else's?'

'Let's leave out the political discussions for now. Of all people, you, I think, communicated quite closely with our opponents. But besides all this, "we" were also understood that the setback from Gush Katif would inevitably lead to Hamas' power, if not in the entire autonomous region, then in Gaza for sure. With all the consequences coming, or to be exact, flying out in the form of Qassam rockets.

'That means that it's you, or rather your rulers that I need to thank for the death of my sons,' Hamid whispered wistfully.

'Thank yourself for voting for Hamas,' Moshe replied roughly.

Hamid glanced at him in surprise. He hadn't seen Moshe like that before. Even after finishing Schroder, he - and this struck Hamid a little less than his very appearance - retained a good-natured expression, and here... there were clenched teeth, his jaws trembled, and an unexpectedly hard look, like the edge of the hand with which he'd chopped down the former Ulenspiegel.

"Hmmm... It's too early to relax. You can't read another man's soul, especially if it's the soul of a Jew."

'Okay, okay, keep listening. After the army and police blocked the borders of Gush Katif on the orders of Sharon to prevent us, the sympathisers from coming to the settlements and disrupting this disengagement plan, tens of thousands of people decided to break through there on a grand scale. At first, we gathered in the small village of Kfar Maimon, near the border of Gush Katif. We wanted to move in a column, but were actually locked right in that settlement. Then, two weeks later, we gathered in Sderot, so that from there we could move in several groups to Gush Katif.'

'To Gaza,' clarified Hamid, who was provoked by Moshe's revelations to express an uncharacteristic stubbornness.

'No,' this time Moshe reacted tolerantly. 'We left Gaza in the nineties. And the majority of the settlements of Gush Katif were situated along the perimeter of Gaza. So, please stop.'

'Then what happened?' Hamid asked quietly, looking at the line of paired red lights dashing past along the right side of the highway and the yellow lights rushing towards them.

'Then? Then, I discover a certain personality in our group that really stood out. Not only were there young people there besides me, but this one was over forty, and he didn't even know a word of Hebrew. We were introduced ourselves to each other. It turned out that he was a German who had nothing to do with Israel. He'd come to Israel specifically to participate in the fight against "Disengagement." His name was Peter; Peter Bigelbauer. "Oh, what wonderful youth you have," he kept saying, admiringly following the marching squad of guys and girls from Bnei Akiva. "How much love for the Motherland, how much courage and spirituality. We have nothing like this in Europe!"

'And what brought him there?' Hamid asked with hostility. 'Christian views or a guilt complex before the Jews?'

'Well, obviously, I didn't ask him about the latter, and he wasn't very talkative about it either. But as regards Christianity, his views are quite curious. He said: "I don't belong to any particular sect. According to my views, I'm a biblical Christian." I think then: "Wow! That's something new." And he clarifies: "The problem is that when Christianity came out of the Bible, it went so far away from it. For all of these two thousand years, it's been politicised far too much. I think that its main task now is to become biblical again."'

'This is especially interesting for me,' Hamid smirked.

'Ah, right,' Moshe winked at him in the mirror. 'What's it for you? We and the Christians are infidels for you. We need to be either banned, squeezed, or both.'

'Why are you saying this?' Hamid mumbled shyly. 'Am I some Hamas's guy, huh?'

'Former,' Moshe cut him off. Hamid wanted to become offended, but then Moshe continued. 'I asked: "Where did you stay in Israel?" And he replied: "What do you mean? I'm staying right here. These are all my clothes." At this he pointed at a backpack which was no bigger than a plastic bag one uses for groceries in a supermarket. Well, anyway, the breakthrough didn't happen for us. Peter and I were among the first to be arrested when we were crawling under the barbed wire. They didn't even check our IDs — they stuffed us into a "zinzan" and took us to the Ashkelon area, not far from that gas station where I first met you. So, I took a taxi and brought him to my place, just like I did with you. We chatted all night long. And a month and a half later, I received a translation of his sketches about his Israeli adventures, and one-third of the narrative was about my humble persona. This was nine years ago. Since then, the internet has flourished, and Peter has become quite successful. He moved with the times, if not to say "hopped" together with the times, and made the intellectual world enjoy his own channel - the internet TV channel. The studio is located in Munich, where we're now headed. The number of daily visits to this channel amounts to tens, if not hundreds of thousands, so the late Schroder is not a competitor to him in terms of popularity. By the way, thanks to Peter, I got here on time. He found me the address of this Schroder in no time. When you ran away, I decided to follow you to the airport in case I could stop you, you fool! It wasn't possible, of course, it was not possible... But while I was driving, YOUR...'

Hamid cringed at this 'your...'

'Your guys bombed my house. So, it turns out, I owe you my life. I got in touch with Peter. Apparently, he knew this Schroder well, that rare bastard. So it happened that I dashed to rescue my saviour, to save my lifesaver.'

'Ulenspiegel,' Hamid whispered, and a wave of unexpected bitterness overwhelmed him.

Hamid was crying, silently and tearlessly. He was lamenting for... no, not for Schroder, but for his dream of meeting the strange and wonderful Ulenspiegel, that Mahdi who turned out to be Dajjal, Satan's servant.

It seemed that Moshe guessed his thoughts.

'What can we do, my dear friend?' he said sadly. 'No matter how beautiful the flowers are in spring, sooner or later they wither. The same happens with our hopes... and what are those Gog and Magog over there?'

A giant black off-roader drew in line with the Audi and started cutting in front of it. At the same time, the right front window lowered down, and our characters saw a man with a gun in his hands.

'Gamal!' Hamid shouted in horror, recognising

his nemesis in the darkness.

Of course, Moshe didn't know who Gamal was, but he evaluated the situation immediately. Sharply accelerating, smashing the hell out of the jeep's side-view mirror and getting a deep scratch on Audi as a souvenir from the sharp edge of the jeep's front light, Moshe grasped the opportunity which appeared in about four hundred meters and took a right at the next exit from the highway.

Bang! Bang! Blam! Bang! Blam! The bullets sent after them didn't reach their goal, and while Gamal's jeep passed the turnoff and was desperately trying to make a U-turn to continue the pursuit, Moshe revved into gear and disappeared without a trace.

'Son of an ass!' Gamal roared, buffeted by the wind on the empty night highway. 'Son of a whore! I fucked your grandmother! I wish you were dipped in shit! I wish my God would curse your father! I wish my God destroyed your house! That's… alright, alright… I'll get to you.'

He grabbed his mobile phone and literally started banging on the screen with his fingers.

'Come on, connect already, son of offal! Ahmed, disease on your dick! Pick up the frigging phone already! Hello, hello, Ahmed? Audi A6… Blue, looks like it's going towards Munich.'

Though it wasn't exactly so.

'Why did we turn?' asked Hamid.

'Because the Stuttgart-Munich route is closed for us now; completely closed.'

'That is…' Hamid was confused.

'I gather your friend isn't alone and has already informed his comrades about us,' Moshe smirked. 'So, if you don't want some new encounters like the one that we just had, then…'

'Does that mean we're not going to Munich now?' Hamid muttered, completely lost.

'We're going, we're going,' he was comforted. 'Only now we'll go by the turns of the corkscrew and get into the city not from the north-west, that is from Stuttgart, but from the north-north-east, from Munich airport side.'

***

He was all somewhat square, that Herr Braun, the police investigator smoking those nasty cigarettes and looking at Marion with his square eyes. His head was square too, and his ears and his jaws, the whole body, even his arms bent at the elbows at exact right angles.

'Yes, I am Marion Bunzen, year of birth — nineteen-ninety, married to Fritz Bunzen, and I work at the hotel Hamburg. I want to understand why you called and summoned me in the middle of the night and…'

'Frau Bunzen,' the detective roared in a bass tone which was intermingled now and then with rattling noise, making Braun's voice sound somewhat square too. 'Frau Bunzen, as the editor of *Neue Stuttgarter Zeitung*, Herr Zitterbakke informed us, as recently as six days ago you came to the office of the newspaper at Schloßstraße 17, and after twenty minutes you cadged - but what am I saying - forcefully tore information from him about the place of residence of the journalist Herman Schroder, who is published under the penname "Ulenspiegel." Could you explain why you needed this?'

'No, I couldn't,' Marion announced, shaking her head with determination, the black waterfall of her hair pouring on her shoulders with renewed vigour. 'I couldn't because it's my personal business. You can reckon that I'm in love with that Ulenspiegel and am going to sleep with him? Are you satisfied with such an answer?'

'Not really,' the broken line of a crooked sneer crossed his square face.

'Huh?'

'Well, first of all, you're married…'

'That's not a problem for me,' this confession combined with the smile on her scarlet lips roused in the policeman an acute desire to bite into those lips with his clean-cut square mouth. Having suppressed that desire - at least for a while - he continued:

'Secondly, it looks like you're not one of those who lets the grass grow under feet, so, if you had such a desire, you would have accomplished it during these six days.'

'And who says I haven't? And again, it's none of your business. I'll do it whenever I want.'

'Well, that's unlikely to happen,' Braun spoke in his spiteful bass, 'Unless you're a necrophile.'

'What do you mean?' Marion frowned.

'The thing is,' Braun pronounced solemnly, his voice rising slightly because of his overwhelming delight, 'that Herr Herman Schroder, pseudonym "Ulenspiegel" was killed a few hours ago near his house in Esslingen. And not only him…'

***

All his life, Hamid had suffered from insomnia. Any trifle, any reason for anxiety could make him toss and turn in his bed until morning. And here, for the first time in his life, in the most probably critical moment, being pursued by terrorists, driving into uncertainty in Moshe's rented Audi A6, suddenly, he, as they say, conked out. And how! Without dreams! As if sinking into the ocean.

He was dragged from that ocean of his by a neon sign, "Freising-suid." And his first thought was — a lighthouse; a lighthouse that was illuminating the ocean at night. White letters on blue... Freising... southern Freising, where probably thousands or maybe tens of thousands of people lived, and none of them knew there was a Hamid Shafi who was being followed by killers and that this Hamid desperately needed help otherwise he would die, and he didn't want to die at all. Strange, right?

And Germans would then, as they are kind, those Germans, right, because they got rid of all the bad ones after World War II? All of them, well, maybe except for that vicious albino old woman, though maybe she was kind too, only dumb. And the Germans would come out of their houses and stand in a crowd as a shield to protect him, Hamid, from that evil Gamal.

There was a turn to some place called Autstart. Alright, Freising was already behind them, whatever, forget about that Freising. "I wish we could turn to that Autstart, hide there, and... Gamal would never find him there." But Moshe was pushing on the accelerator relentlessly.

'Arena,' he unexpectedly announced with a hoarse

sound from his long silence voice.

'What?' Hamid asked, following with his eyes the passing and disappearing behind his back lit carcass of a gigantic pink whale.

'The Arena Stadium.'

***

The modular camera looked straight at Hamid. It looked like it was alive. Hamid had slept in the studio for several hours, but never fully regained consciousness.

'Get up! Now it's prime time!'

He tried to look away, but lanky Peter, standing behind the cameraman, made terrible faces at him and waved his hands constantly as if saying, "look at the camera."

'My name is Hamid Shafi. I came from Gaza via Israel to Germany using a fake passport with the name Hamid Kulani…'

He felt as if his larynx was being scratched with glass dust. His words were tearing out all ragged and bloody. Every adjective, it seemed, left a crack on his lips, every interjection a burn on the tongue.

'There!' Hamid shouted, pulling the Instruction

from under his shirt and unfolding it in front of the camera. 'There: this is the Instruction! These are the regulations on the application of fire within the city limits that belonged to the Hamas brigade Shudjaia. I got it…' Hamid almost blurted out that he'd received it from Sari Al-Farane, with whom he'd spent time in prison, from Sari, a consistent fighter against Hamas, an inveterate Fatah adept, Abu-Mazen's friend. 'Right here! I mean, it's put down in black and white: "The civil population of Gaza must be used against the IDF as the latter strives to minimise losses among the civil population." Right here, do you hear me? "Zionists must limit the use of weapons for the sake of diminishing losses among civilians of the enclave, therefore it is difficult for them to get the maximum from their weapon and firearms." And also — "The presence of civilians creates a number of resistance zones to the advancement of IDF forces that would lead to the following difficulties: at opening fire; at controlling the civil population during and after operations, and providing medical aid for civilians." And then further — "there is no doubt the gains we will receive with maximum losses among civilians and the destruction of infrastructure. The main advantage of this is the growth of a negative sentiment towards the IDF and, accordingly, increased support for the forces of resistance."'

Hamid's voice became stronger. Looking into the black eye of the camera, he started speaking about the circumstances of how his wife and children died, how he was manhandled in prison, how his friends were killed, and how he was trying to reach Schroder in Stuttgart, and how he finally met him.

'I mean, then,' Hamid continued, 'I realised that this man, Schroder, was not only not Ulenspiegel, not only a liar ear-bashing about his compassion for our miserable people while there was no compassion at all; oh no, I realised something even more significant. I understood that this particular pseudo-Ulenspiegel was the main reason why my children died. Yes, right, not Hamas at all, but he specifically and the likes to him are the real commissioners of the peaceful civilians' deaths because their deaths give all of those so-called left and liberal scribblers the opportunity to do business on our blood, and at the same time to spread their anti-Semite Nazi nonsense. Yes, I realised all that, but it was too late. Schroder's handyman was already tightening his garrotte around my throat. And here is another instruction. It's not that secret, but interesting nonetheless. It was issued by the Ministry of Internal Affairs and National Security of Palestinian autonomy.

1. Any deceased person should be first of all be called a "civilian," Hamid started reading, 'and only

then can you mention his status in the jihad or military rank. Do not forget to always add "an innocent citizen" or "a civilian" to the name of the deceased.

2. Start your reports on attacks by the Palestinian opposition with the phrase: "In response to the cruel Israeli aggression," and finish it with the phrase: "Such-and-such number of people have died since the beginning of the Israeli aggression in Gaza". Always follow the formula "the attack is in response to the occupation -Palestinians only react."

3. Follow the reports of Israeli representatives. Always discredit them, defy them, and present them as a lie.

4. Avoid the publications of photographs of missiles launched into Israel from the residential districts of Gaza. Do not publish photographs of places where the fire is on.

5. Do not publish photographs of our soldiers in masks and with heavy weaponry so that we are not accused of instigating violence.

6. When communicating with Western journalists, use rational political language, and avoid emotional outbursts. Our goal is to expose the villainy of occupation and condemn it as violence.

7. Do not try to persuade Western people that the Holocaust was a lie. Do not deny the Catastrophe. On

the contrary, use it for comparison to show that right now, Israel is doing the same thing to the Palestinians.

8. Use the narrative of life against the narrative of blood. When you are talking to Arabs, speak of the deceased as martyrs who fell in actions with the aggressors, but when you are talking to the Western people, speak of the deceased as peaceful citizens. Speak about the huge number of the wounded. Show the human face of the Palestinian sufferings. Vividly describe ordeals of the peaceful residents under the oppression of occupation and bombings.

9. Do not publish photographs of military commanders. Do not mention their names and do not praise their successes during conversations with foreign friends.'

Ba-bang! Bounce went the door from its hinges and fell on the floor with a crash!

'Stay where you are! Hands in the air!'

Upon seeing the police and the barrels of their guns, Hamid and Moshe obediently raised their arms. Even before that, Peter had done the same thing, his arms rising somewhat strangely, as if with a jerk, like a puppet or a windup doll. The only person who didn't obey was the camera operator, who became a little agitated at the sight of cops. He directed his camera at them, and adjusted the microphone so the audience could better hear what the guardians of the order were going to say. At one point, the muzzle of one of the machine guns and the operator's camera were staring at each other, like some sort of silent duel. And then the policeman yelled at the operator:

'Switch off the camera!'

"Why would I do that?" the camera operator wondered, and continued to broadcast the puffy, bewildered face of the policeman to thousands of admiring spectators.

'I don't understand what is going on,' Peter Bigelbauer said, suddenly coming back to his senses, his arms turning from being obediently raised arms into two question marks. 'Why are you intruding into a studio where representatives of the free media work? Do we live in the Third Reich, or maybe the Soviet Union?'

'We are here,' the policeman pronounced, "to fulfil the order of the head of the Bavarian Land Criminal Department, Mr Rauschenbach, to detain Moshe Nissan and Hamid Kuilani.'

'I mean, I am Shafi!' Hamid shouted.

'…as suspects in the murder of Rasem Al-Rimavi, Abbas Nadji, Mahmud Hemeid, and Herman Schroder. Before the investigation is complete, according to the law, it's prohibited to disclose any details about it.

I demand you remove the cameras immediately and warn all those present about their responsibility as regards the disclosure of the secrets of the investigation.'

'We don't have any secrets from our audience!' Peter exclaimed. 'Continue, Hamid!'

At that moment, with the agility of a commando and by no means that of a sixty-four-year-old man, Moshe rushed into the corridor and disappeared into its dark trench, dragging the guardians of order with him, and Hamid, taking advantage of the confusion, spoke quickly:

'I want you, Europeans, to know that the killers of our people are not in Tel Aviv at all, and not even in Gaza. The murderers of our people are here in Europe. They are those who declare themselves fighters for our people's rights. And I... what about me? The enemies who wanted to kill me killed each other - Rasmi...'

'Who?' Peter asked him to clarify.

'I mean, Rasem... Rasem was killed by Abbas and Mahmud — they stabbed him, and Abbas and Mahmud were shot by Schroder...'

'And what about Schroder?' shouted the police captain, reappearing in the room and pointing the muzzle of his gun at Hamid.

Then he burst into a tirade in German, addressing the operator. Although Hamid didn't understand a word, the point of the tirade was perfectly clear: the cameraman was being instructed to remove his damn camera if he didn't want the damn camera to be blasted to hell by gunfire.

'Is this called democracy?' the operator retorted calmly, focusing his camera on his opponent.

The opponent couldn't find the words to reply, and switching to Hamid spoke in bad English:

'So, the program is over. Messrs Bigelbauer, Nissan, and Kulaini, I request you to follow me.'

'Provide the general warrant,' Mr. Bigelbauer announced. 'Otherwise, your actions are not lawful, and I'm not going anywhere.'

Mr Kulaini was silent, and instead of him Mr Shafi responded boldly:

'Then let that Kulaini go with you; but I am Shafi!'

Mr Nissan, in the meantime, was heroically fighting with the policemen who were trying to capture him in the depths of that studio.

***

'Hello? Yeah, Monira, yes-yes, it's me, Gamal. What? What computer? I don't understand. They're speaking? Hamid? Are you sure it's the same Hamid? What's his last name? Right, Hamid Shafi. Yes, from Gaza, from Shudjaia, to be precise. That's right. And who's with him? I'm asking who the second guy is. What? I can't believe my ears! This can't be true! So, who cares if he's an Israeli? Maybe he's an Israeli Arab? Could that Hamid be in cahoots with a Jew? A disease on his dick! Ah, he is a Zionist whore, a faggot's brother. Now I understand why he took care of Mahmud, Abbas and Schroder so easily. So, you say they're speaking on the internet television channel? That's where they went. Well, right, we lost them on the highway to Munich... and how long ago did they start? And what, do they blame us for all the crimes? Argh, screw his sister! Monira, call Mustafa quickly — let him find the address of that studio and we'll go there with Farid. What do you mean by "how will you find it?" We'll use the navigation. No, I'm afraid we won't be able to disrupt the interview — Mustafa needs to find everything out yet, and we still need to get to them, and at least punish them as a lesson to everybody else!'

Gamal ended the call and gently stroked his Carl Gustaf rifle. "There, there, buddy, I'm not angry with you for not performing your best there on the highway. It happens. Just don't let me down now.'

A Carl Gustaf was not better than a Kalashnikov, but it had a reach of two hundred metres and emitted six hundred shots per minute, and the fact that this son of a whore Hamid got away together with his Jew, frankly speaking, was not Carl Gustaf's fault, but his own, Gamal's. Why was he begrudging the shells, then? He should have gone at them with bursts rather than firing single shots.

Gamal's mobile sang.

'Hello,' he perked up.

'Write down this address,' said Monira.

***

Hamid stood still. He'd flown across half of Europe and experienced such things, Allah forbid, and all in order to tell the world his story. And now, when his dream had finally come true, when somewhere in the labyrinths of Europe thousands or tens of thousands of faces were clinging to their computer screens, they expect that after his confused accusatory monologue, he, having told in detail what had happened, told what he witnessed and what his children had become the victims of, now he would speak about how Hamas's people followed those silent, sometimes not even pronounced out loud instructions of the fine folks from European editorial offices and television studios and from the headquarters of numerous organisations fighting for the ideals of humanism in words, but in deeds for a new Auschwitz.

Everything went to waste.

Hamid didn't move. The silence was so thick one could cut it with a knife, like cheese.

Suddenly, Moshe emerged from the dark corridor, doubled up as both of his arms were twisted behind his back by the two solemnly plodding policemen on his right and left. At that, the police captain started shaking with indignation.

'Ah, Mr Nissan? Now we'll go to the police station, and there you'll definitely share with us how you turned up in Germany. What are you doing here if you're a citizen of Israel?'

'What am I doing?' Moshe raised his head immediately. 'What am I doing? I can tell, I can tell you right here; I'm here because of Hamid! Back home in Israel, Hamid saved my life. Unwittingly, but he did. I was sure what that Schroder would be, that "Ulenspiegel" - let the memory of him be cursed - I wanted to dissuade, to change Hamid's mind. I didn't manage to shatter his illusions, and then he ran away. So, there was only one thing for me to do — to follow him to Germany and save him from that damned Schroder.'

The English word 'damned' Moshe pronounced with such a savoury tone it was as if it was melting in his mouth. And then there was a pause. There was supposed to be a confession to murder, even with extenuating circumstances, but murder. And were there any extenuating circumstances or not? It should be checked and double-checked, as, at the moment, there were four corpses in play and only one apparent murderer — Moshe Nissan.

'Entschuldigen Sie mir bitte! Das Tur war geoffnet!'

If Hamid knew German, he would have understood that a tall man in a jacket that seemed as if it had just been ironed, in a white shirt, a blue tie, and a grey hat had suddenly entered the room. He had a short beard and a somewhat piercing look — a look under which one wanted to stand bolt upright and cry out: 'I repent! In sins as in burdocks! But Allah is my witness — I won't do it again!' Apologising for his unexpected appearance and explaining that the door was open, the gentleman introduced himself:

'Friedrich Schwartz. Ein Rechtsanwalt. A lawyer,'

he clarified, turning to Moshe and then to Hamid.

'A lawyer?' Moshe repeated.

'Yes,' he nodded. 'Herman Schroder's lawyer.'

The head of the police task force interrupted their conversation with the wildest tirade of abuses in German addressed at his subordinates, who stood there with their heads bowed, though still holding Moshe's wrists. Apparently, he was reprimanding them for leaving the outer door open, which was indeed unforgivable and strangely negligence of the law enforcement officers, as a result of which the stray criminal Moshe could simply escaped if he decided to. The outburst of official indignation ended with a phrase of a clearly imperative nature, after which handcuffs were immediately put on Moshe. After that, the policeman turned to the lawyer.

'*Was willst du?*'

'*Nicht was willst du, aber was wollen Sie.*'

'*Was wollen Sie?*'

Completely ignoring him, the rogue lawyer addressed Moshe, Hamid, and the numerous audience members who were delightedly following what was happening on the screens of their TVs all around Europe and across the ocean.

'The late Herr Schroder,' he announced in perfect English without an accent, 'a few hours before his tragic death, trusting neither the ordinary post that could be snatched away, nor electronic mail that could be hacked, came personally to me, extremely excited; he kept saying he had a serious conflict with Hamas, and that Hamas' soldiers had some problems with him and wanted to kill him, and that he'd been driving around Bavaria for an hour in order to ascertain that there were no grey men following him. And that this is the USB drive that contains an interview with a man from Gaza, the man whose children died because of Hamas, and that he would warn Hamas that in case of his death this material would be aired on state television. "And indeed," he said, "if they do bump me off," the lawyer added this vivid phrase 'bump off,' with a flourish, "make this interview public. That would be your vengeance for me. Here is the USB drive."'

The captain jumped at the flashcard like a goalie at a ball, but Schwartz immediately moved his hand away and squeezed the precious evidence in it.

'Beware,' he said, looking not at the policeman, but at the blue iris of the TV camera, 'this flashcard is my property, and please, don't stretch your filthy hands at it.'

The captain barked something in German.

'You're saying that it's an evidential matter?' the lawyer asked again in his beautiful English, obviously playing to the international crowd. 'Okay, then show me the warrant resolution on withdrawal and I'll give this precious evidence to you with pleasure. Well?'

And again, in front of the viewers, he dangled the flashcard in front of the captain. The latter waved his hands indecisively, while his fingers curled up by themselves, as if with each hand he was trying to catch a tennis ball that had fallen from the sky. It was evident he was struggling with an almost irresistible desire to snatch the coveted item from the hands of the vile pen-pusher but did not dare, realising that such lawlessness, especially before the eyes of the whole world, would instantly end his career.

'Well? No warrant?' Friedrich Schwartz goaded him. 'Then I am sorry.'

He walked up to the cameraman with huge steps and with the words: 'Please show this material to our dear viewers,' solemnly handed him the flashcard.

***

With a shout of '*Nein*,' the captain dashed at him again and, sputtering, started speaking in German.

'What does the secrecy of the investigation have to do with it?' the lawyer said in English with astonishment. 'It's mine, and until I'm provided with the statement on withdrawal, I can do whatever I want with it.' And then, turning back to the operator, he proudly commanded: 'Insert and open it!'

He knew that after his performance on TV today, he'd secured new clients for many years ahead.

'March the detained away,' the captain commanded gloomily, staring at the floor.

The procession moved towards the door. Hamid was leading the procession, then there was the captain with the gun in his hand, and the two policemen with Moshe between them bringing up the rear.

'Hey, dearest,' the lawyer suddenly addressed the back of the departing captain in English. 'Why don't you take those handcuffs off Mr Nissan? It's no good to put such accessories on an innocent person. And you'll have to take them off, anyway. Until then, he won't run away because he has nowhere to go. Am I right, Mr Nissan?'

Moshe nodded.

'Don't you worry, both of you are going to be free soon — I'm personally going to take your case, so I guarantee that it won't even go to court.'

'Take off the handcuffs,' the captain ordered almost inaudibly.

***

This had happened to Hamid a few times already. Some invisible hammer started knocking nails in the nape of his neck, invisible but sharp… or maybe, on the contrary, blunt. Of course, blunt, heavy, massive, so that his entire head was thumping. The first time it had happened was when he and Aya and the children were swimming near the shore… Eh, but for Hamas's people, it could have been such a great resort in Gaza — like Dubai. …And the Jews had left already — create as much as you want! But it's easier to kill than build, and if the entire world is shouting to your people decade after decade: 'Jews are evil!' Well, how can one not believe this world?

***

Aya swam underwater and then emerged. Hamid glanced at her, and he was as if burnt by the beauty of his beloved one. Her wet hair was running down her shoulders like black springs, her big grey eyes like a rumiya's were like two bunnies under the fur of her eyelashes, and her lips… once, their neighbour Liana, who was so mean, had commented, asking why she was using such a bright lipstick... and she didn't have any make-up on at all. That was his Aya — his princess, a princess from One Thousand and One Nights, his princess Budur!

This is how he admired Aya, swimming with her, and when he got out of the water, it was as if someone hit him with a spade on the back of the head with all their might. At the time, he didn't understand what it was. And then he drank a coffee and almost died. That's when he realised — it was his blood pressure. Only there was nowhere to measure it on the beach. And once again, his blood pressure rose when he sat with Taufik, smoking and drinking coffee. Taufik had a device, but it was faddish... It showed two hundred over one hundred. Then Taufik measured his blood pressure. It also showed two hundred. They measured Taufik's little daughter, Sabira, — two hundred over one hundred. Then they realised the device was out of order. Aisha, Taufik's wife, ran to the neighbours in search of a normal device while Hamid was groaning. The feeling was no longer a hammer and nails, but as if they were hitting the back of the head with gunfire from an M-16. Then Taufik gave him vazodip — a pressure medicine which is Israeli, by the way.

'Well, okay,' he joked, 'the more we drink, the less

the Jews will have.'

Aisha arrived with a good blood pressure monitor, and when they measured it, it turned out to be one-hundred-and-thirty-eight over eighty-nine.

'The lower one, frankly, is high,' Sari said with concern, 'and the top – one-hundred-and-thirty-eight, frankly, it's too much high.'

But what the pressure at the peak of the pain in the back of the head was remained unknown.

The third time it happened, he was at home. His caring Aya had brought a blood pressure monitor from the hospital where she worked a while ago. It showed one-hundred-and-fifty over ninety. Hamid realised that the problem with high blood pressure was serious. And then the war started… and the illness was gone. It seemed as if his body had told itself: "There is no time for that now." And the headaches disappeared, though they came back a couple of times when he was in prison — not as the hammer with nails or the M-16, but with some clout. The Hamas's jailers were hitting much harder. And now, as they were leaving the studio and stepping onto the dark staircase, they suddenly started shooting into Hamid's nape again. And how! Even the police captain who was walking next to him, without lowering his gun muzzle as they came to an electric light under a marquee, asked: 'What are you making faces for?'

Hamid was not making faces. He was squirming in sync with the pulsing in his nape, which felt like the onset of a stroke. The stroke didn't happen, though, as it was outrun by the burst from the bushes opposite the entrance, as a result of which Hamid felt pain in his stomach and chest much stronger than the one reigning at the back of his head. He didn't even have time to understand why his legs stopped carrying him, why they started shambling on the asphalt, why that asphalt was approaching his face so fast, and the beige wall of the house which had been painted fairly recently by the look of it, together with the shiny white marquee were floating somewhere up. Curled up by the next burst, the police captain strangely doubled as if starting some dance, flipped his arms up abruptly, at which his gun flew up before clanking powerfully onto the asphalt right at Moshe's feet. But the captain thought twice about his dance — he just made an anxious pirouette, and then, as if tripping, stretched out next to the bleeding Hamid.

Moshe and the policemen fell on the ground, so the next two volleys flew over their heads. If only the unknown shooters that were hiding in the bushes were snipers they could have easily liquidated the three remaining rascals, as they were well lit by the bright lamp, thus very easy targets. But they were not snipers, and because their victims didn't return fire that made them feel safe, and they jumped up and, shooting on the way, ran towards the entrance. They shouldn't have done that. The policemen were indeed paralysed and none of them even tried to unbuckle their holsters, but Moshe, plopping with his slightly protruding belly at the age of sixty-four on the captain's gun, revived the feeling of once having been a SWAT soldier. He took the gun, the new Heckler&Koch P-2000, and released the safety catch. Covered by the noise of the machine gun, his single shots weren't even discernible. Besides, as they were falling, the attackers kept on shooting, though without any results, and only when their souls flew away to the embraces of the notorious virgins, did their fingers finally release the triggers. The guardians of order arose to the cooling bodies of the gunmen as Moshe screamed: 'Ambulance! Ambulance!'

Obediently, the police began to call — one for an ambulance, and the other to his superiors. Moshe rushed to Hamid, who was lying in a pool of blood.

'Well, that's it...' Hamid whispered, blood bubbling on his lips.

'Hamid, Hamid!' It seemed to Moshe that he was whispering, but in fact, he continued to yell. 'You saved my life! I rushed after you to Germany to save you, and I failed!'

'Well, the winds don't blow the way the ships want…' Hamid's whisper weakened with every second. 'Everything is fine… Nothing keeps me in this reserve of Shaitan. Everyone I loved is already there.'

'Hamid,' Moshe wheezed in despair.

'Thank you, Moshe,' was the barely audible reply. What Hamid was trying to say could hardly even be distinguished by the movement of his lips. 'You helped me a lot. Allah is wise, and he sent you to me. Thanks to you, I accomplished what I had to do; thanks to you, my sufferings obtained a meaning. Now the whole world will know…'

"Yeah, right, as if the world needs to know. The world, this stinky world, everybody knows anyway — so what? It's ready to send millions of Arabic children to perish if only it leads to the death of millions of Jews!" Moshe wanted to say bitterly, but there was nobody to say this to…

The dawn was breaking. The streetlights were like day-fly dragonflies setting off on their last flight, which was destined to last only for a few final moments before the thrifty Germans turned off the electricity. In the park, which began some forty metres from the entrance, a nightingale's qaddish on the departed righteous man, one of the righteous peoples of the world,

Hamid — son of Ibrahim, was stretched out. Strengthening, the rays of the sun stroked the verdure, which was chartreuse in spring but had long since become dark green, mossy green, and was now preparing to try on yellow, emerald, and fulvous colours.

"I do not believe that a person disappears completely after death, and Muslim stories about seventy-two houri are ridiculous to me. But somewhere my Hamid had to find shelter and peace. He deserved it for his sufferings."

***

Exactly thirty days after Hamid's soul left his bullet-riddled body, a beer festival called Oktoberfest was taking place in Munich - THE BIGGEST FOLK HOLIDAY OF THE WORLD. Its history began over two-hundred-years-ago, on October 12th, 1810, during the festivities on the occasion of the marriage of the Crown Prince, the future King of Bavaria Ludwig I, and Princess Teresa of Saxony Hildburhausen. The festivities ended on October 17th in a meadow named after Princess Teresa. The residents of Munich residents now call it Wiesen for short, which translates as 'meadow.'

At first, beer was sold in small stalls, the number of which increased every year. Then, in 1896, there appeared big pavilions erected by the owners of Munich's beerhouses and breweries. Since then and until today, all the beer that is consumed during Oktoberfest must be produced solely in Bavaria, just like the snacks that were served on the oak tables standing in those pavilions — white sausages with boiled pork guts - Weisswurst, delicious pretzels - Brezels and Süßer Senf — sweet mustard. A carousel and two swings sprouted up next to the pavilions. This is how the Oktoberfest Superland was founded, which now delights children and adults with a rollercoaster, one of the fastest in the world, and a Freefall Tower, a device which falls from a height of seventy meters, and other attractions.

In 2014, the Oktoberfest lasted from September 20th to October 5th. On one of the nights, as already reported, exactly thirty days after the death of Hamid, Marion and Fritz Bunzen arrived in Munich in their Opel Astra. As they approached the hotel where they'd reserved a room, Marion noticed an absolutely immobile man lying on the lawn in the shabby light of the streetlamps.

'Dead,' she asked, appalled, 'or homeless?'

'Oktoberfest,' her husband replied through gritted teeth. 'It's about three hundred meters from our hotel… And this one,' he made a gesture with his head as if he wanted to turn around, 'didn't make it to his shelter.'

As it turned out, some Oktoberfest guests didn't have a place to sleep at all. Among the countless Munich hobos, the well-dressed, clean-shaven guys clearly stood out, resting their boisterous heads on their neat backpacks containing, obviously, three or four changes of underwear and a toothbrush. So, what could they do? Up to 6,000,000 people come to Munich for the holiday, and for the majority, a hotel falls into the realm of vague dreams. First come, first served. And you want a beer, especially since it's prepared with a special, increased strength for Oktoberfest.

This last fact was especially noticeable. The guy lying on the lawn was only the first sign. That night at the hotel was not the calmest one. Until one in the morning, a stirring chorus rang from the beerhouse next door, in which the windows - on the fourth floor - were trembling, and drunken shouts were heard from the streets until dawn.

That morning, after making love and having breakfast, they headed for Teresa's meadow. Along the way, they came across cafés and pubs with tables right on the streets, and everywhere at these tables sat Bavarians in leather shorts and cowboy checkered shirts with suspenders who were rattling their glass litre mugs and consuming beer. Some were crowned with characteristic hats with feathers protruding from them.

In anticipation of the concert scheduled for 11am, Marion and Fritz went into one of the large beer pavilions. In the centre, an orchestra played on a raised platform. A dancer in traditional Bavarian clothes performed a dance with shepherd's whips. Then the melody "Happy birthday to you!" started playing, and the entire hall joined in. Hundreds of people congratulated one person, a complete stranger. At the right moment, the man on the dais inserted the name. Bavarians are one family.

The spouses sat at the oak table and ordered a litre mug of beer each. Next to them sat a young man with a charming girl, both wearing Bavarian clothes. They were kissing now and then, as is normal in public places in Munich. At one point in their conversation, it looked like they had a fight. The girl got up and, snapping something rude over her shoulder, left. The guy was sitting alone, but not for long. Having finished his beer, he stepped away somewhere and in fifteen minutes was back… with a new girl. They ordered more beer and then… the first girl returned with a new young man. There was no harsh bicker fest there — Bavaria is not Spain, so they all started drinking beer peacefully.

'It seems that in Munich now, people's whole lives are spent in beer pavilions,' Marion whispered into her husband's ear. 'I wouldn't be surprised if they have sex on the oak tables now.'

'It's fine,' Fritz replied in a whisper. 'As soon as Oktoberfest is over, everything will be fine.'

At a quarter to eleven, our couple hurried to the statue of Bavaria for the concert. Several ensembles and wind orchestras started playing the national anthem of Bavaria, and people started singing in unison:

'Gott mit dir, du Land der Bayern,
deutsche Erde, Vaterland!
Über deinen weiten Gauen
ruhe seine Segenshand!
|: Er behüte deine Fluren,
schirme deiner Städte Bau
und erhalte dir die Farben
seines Himmels, weiß und blau!'

'Let the Almighty cherish you,
Oh, Bavaria, my land!
Let he bless the fields of yours,
All those free and spacious lands!
Width of splendid brightest meadows,
Walls of all the little towns,
And the colours of our sky

That are always blue and white!'

After singing the anthem, according to the local tradition, hundreds of colourful balloons flew up into the sky. They were floating away, so light, like multi-coloured human souls. And then, something inexplicable happened — one of the balloons got separated from the flock and began to decline sharply. Scurrying in the air, it landed on Marion's shoulder, who was taken aback by it. It started rubbing itself on her cheek like a cat, and Marion felt as if it had a human's breath. She didn't realise what she was doing, but Marion embraced its warm body and touched its gentle surface with her lips.

'Shukra,' she heard a whisper from nowhere. She didn't know what it meant, but for some reason, her eyes welled up with tears. And the balloon soared up high and somersaulting, headed for the sky. It was in a hurry.

Quick! Join your family!